DRASTIC CRIMES CALL FOR DRASTIC INSIGHTS

PIPER ASHWELL PSYCHIC P.I., BOOK 3

KELLY HASHWAY

Copyright © 2019 Kelly Hashway
All rights reserved.

This is a work of fiction. Any resemblance to actual places or people, living or dead, is entirely coincidental. No part of this book may be reproduced, copied, or recorded without written permission from the author.

The author acknowledges the trademark status and trademark ownership of all trademarks mentioned in this book. Trademarks are not sponsored or endorsed by the trademark owners.

Cover design ©Red Umbrella Graphic Designs

To Ayla with love

CHAPTER ONE

Mitchell wasn't wrong when he said this case was a doozy. There's no evidence whatsoever. No leads. Nothing. Which is why he brought the case to me. When all else fails, call in the psychic PI.

"Run me through it again," I tell Mitchell.

He adjusts his tie, which isn't part of his usual attire at all, and leans back in the chair on the opposite side of my desk. Then his green eyes focus on me. "Maggie Burns went missing on Thursday night—"

"So two nights ago," I interrupt.

Mitchell nods. "She works at Saves-A-Lot—"

"The discount grocery store on Second Street."

"Do you plan to keep doing that?" Mitchell asks, a hint of annoyance in his voice.

"Careful, Piper, finishing each other's sentences is a sign of—"

I hold up my hand to stop Dad from finishing his statement. His comments about the way Mitchell and I interact are getting old. My relationship with Detective Mitchell Brennan is strictly professional. When he gets a case he can't solve on his own, he asks for my help since I can read the energy off objects and find missing persons, whether they're alive or dead. Mitchell tries to pretend he and I are friends as well as occasional partners in this industry, but I know his desire to work with me stems from the fact that his mother was psychic and despite foreseeing her own death, she did nothing to prevent it. The problem is that makes him try his damnedest to protect me, which couldn't be more annoying.

"Go on, Mitchell," I say, ignoring the smirk on Dad's face.

"Maggie was working late, doing inventory. Her car is still in the parking lot, which indicates something happened to her before she left work."

"She could've gotten a ride from someone she knew. Do you know if she had any car trouble earlier in the day?" I ask.

Mitchell sits up straight in his chair. "Are you asking because you're sensing she did?"

I hold up my right palm. "Have you given me a personal belonging to read?" He knows how this works. I have nothing but a missing persons report. I can't read anything off that.

He stands up and huffs. "Then why don't we head to Saves-A-Lot and check out her employee locker?"

"Now you're thinking," I say, tossing my empty coffee cup into the trash can.

When Dad doesn't get up, I narrow my eyes at him. "Aren't you coming?"

"Nah. You two go on ahead. I'm going to check out Maggie's social media accounts and see if anyone was stalking or threatening her online." He opens his laptop and immediately gets to work.

"Good thinking. We'll let you know what we find out, and keep us updated on anything you find." I give a small wave as Mitchell and I head out of the office.

"Will do," Dad calls after us without looking up from his computer screen.

I'm a little relieved he's not tagging along. Ever since Dad came out of retirement from the Weltunkin PD to work with me, I've been worried about his safety. Our last case, which was our first case together as private investigators, put him in more danger than he'd seen in all his years as a police detective. I can't help feeling responsible.

Mitchell unlocks his Explorer, and as if he's reading my mind, he says, "He'll be fine."

"I know." I peer through the office window to see Dad on his laptop, his eyes squinted in concentration. "It's just that he was abducted from that office less than two weeks ago. It's still fresh on my mind."

"I get that, but what are the odds this case will turn out to be as crazy as our last one?"

"Way to jinx us." I get into the SUV and click my seat belt.

"Do you actually believe in that kind of thing?" he asks as he backs out of the parking spot.

"I have visions, and you're asking if I believe in the ability to jinx something?"

He laughs. "I guess you probably operate under the assumption that anything is possible, huh?"

"You could say that."

Traffic is mild, so it only takes us a few minutes to get to Saves-A-Lot. Despite Maggie's disappearance, the store is open as usual. Mitchell finds a spot near the cart return and parks. He grabs his jacket, shrugging it on before getting out of the car.

"Trying to cover your badge?" I ask as I walk around the front of the car to meet him.

"No need to make people panic." He zips his jacket, and we walk into the store. "We're meeting the manager, a guy named Emit Wilkes. He said we should head to the black double doors in the back and ask for him."

I don't shop in this grocery store, so I'm not exactly familiar with the layout. Despite Weltunkin being a wealthy town, there are some discount stores located on the outskirts like this. Not that I'm wealthy or a snob, but I don't really come to this side of town often. I use the grocery store closest to my apartment building for the sheer convenience. Though, thanks to my job, I typically live on takeout food.

Mitchell seems to know where he's going, so I follow his lead. Near the cases of assorted cuts of meat is a set of double doors. A worker is emerging from them as we approach.

"Excuse me," Mitchell says. "We're supposed to be meeting Emit Wilkes. I'm Detective Brennan, and this is Piper Ashwell." He gestures to me.

The guy, who looks to be in his late teens or early twenties, jerks his thumb over his shoulder. "Yeah, Mr. Wilkes told us all you were coming and to send you on back."

"Thanks," Mitchell says, pushing open one of the doors and holding it for me.

We walk past a doorway that leads to the butcher area on the right. To our left is a storage section with shelves of boxes. And straight ahead appears to be either an office or employee room. We head for that, and Mitchell knocks on the door.

I look around, trying to get a sense of Maggie Burns, but since I've yet to hold anything that belonged to her, I can't put my senses on anything in particular.

A short man with thinning brown hair comes to the door. "Detective Brennan?" he asks Mitchell.

"Yes, and this is my partner, Ms. Ashwell."

"Nice to meet you. Please come inside." Emit Wilkes holds the door open for us, and we step into the employee room. "We can speak in my office." Emit motions to the door on our left.

"Actually, I'd love to see where Maggie kept her belongings while she was working," I say, knowing he'll have nothing more to offer us than what we've already read in the missing persons report.

"Sure. Right this way." Emit brings us to a row of lockers on the back wall. "This one here is Maggie's." He reaches into his pants pocket and produces a set of keys, which he uses to open the locker.

"Thank you," I say, even though I could have opened the locker myself. As soon as I touched the combination lock, I could have called forth a vision of Maggie opening the locker. I also carry a lockpick kit in my purse, but his way is faster, so I don't complain. Still, he doesn't show any signs of leaving us alone, which means I'm going to have to read Maggie's belongings in his presence, and that doesn't make me happy at all.

I peer inside the locker. There's a picture of Maggie and a man in a cheap magnetic frame stuck to the inside of the locker door.

"I take it that's Maggie's husband," Mitchell says.

"Yes. His name is Glen," Emit says. "Nice guy. He always goes to the employee Christmas party each year with Maggie."

Nothing about Glen is setting off my radar, so I move on. A jacket is hanging from the hook beneath the top shelf.

On the shelf is an insulated lunch bag. I opt to try reading the jacket and reach for it.

"Was anyone else here Thursday night with Maggie?" Mitchell asks, and I'm sure he's trying to keep Emit distracted so I can have a vision without being stared at like I'm a freak.

"Yeah, the produce manager was—"

Maggie's standing in front of her locker, her hand reaching for the jacket when her phone rings in her back pocket. She grabs it and stares at the number on the screen. Her brow furrows when she doesn't recognize the caller.

"Who could this be?" She presses the button to answer the call. "Hello?"

Static.

"Hello?" she says again, moving toward the back door. "Stupid reception. Hang on a second." She pushes open the door and steps outside. "Hello?" she says again.

A blunt object connects with the back of her head.

Everything goes black.

CHAPTER TWO

"Piper? Piper?"

I come to on the floor of the employee room, my head in Mitchell's lap.

"How do you feel?" Mitchell asks.

"Like my head's been split down the center." I reach for the back of my head as I sit up.

Mitchell is hesitant to let go of me as he asks, "Maggie?"

Emit eyes me as if unsure if he should call an ambulance since to him it must look like I fainted. "What just happened? Do you need a doctor?"

"No." I get to my feet with some assistance from Mitchell. "Mr. Wilkes, my name is Piper Ashwell. I'm a psychic PI working with the Weltunkin PD. I just had a vision of Maggie Burns getting a phone call on Thursday night. She didn't recognize the number and the line was nothing but static when she answered, so she took the phone outside." My gaze goes to Mitchell. "Then she was hit over the head."

"Are you saying she was attacked?" Emit asks, sounding

more surprised by that than by the fact that I just saw what happened to Maggie.

"That's exactly what I'm saying, which means we need access to the footage from your security cameras. I'm assuming you have them in the back lot as well as the front."

Emit's brow furrows. "Well, the cameras are there, but they aren't functioning. They're more to deter people from trying to steal."

"They don't actually work." Mitchell's comment is more of a grumble of disappointment than anything else.

"Then we'll need a list of every employee that was still here that night at…" What time was on her phone display? I close my eyes and recall the image. "11:43."

"I'll go check the employee schedule now. Give me one moment." Emit disappears inside his office, not bothering to close the door behind him.

"You okay?" Mitchell asks me.

"Fine."

"Then why are you pressing your hand against the top of your head?"

"To keep it from splitting in two." I let out a deep breath. I'd take some aspirin, but doing so makes it tough to have visions and there may be more for me to read in Maggie's locker.

Mitchell's giving me that sympathetic look he's gotten so good at over the past several weeks. I hate it.

"Don't."

"I wasn't going to say anything."

"I don't have to touch you to know you're lying through your teeth." I turn away from him and go back to Maggie's locker.

"Piper, don't try to read anything else. You clearly need to recuperate from the vision you just had."

DRASTIC CRIMES CALL FOR DRASTIC INSIGHTS

I ignore him and grab the lunch bag from the shelf. Before trying to read it, I peek inside since the weight alone tells me it's not empty. On the bottom of the bag is a small red apple.

"What is it?" Mitchell asks.

"What's left of her dinner, I guess." Something about the apple bothers me, though. I reach for it, but Emit returns from his office.

"Here you are. A list of all the employees who were working Thursday night. As you'll see, many were on the same schedule as Maggie, so they would have still been here at 11:43."

"Thank you," Mitchell says, taking the list from Emit. "Piper, you about ready?"

"Yeah." I stare at the apple, and one thought pops into my mind: *forbidden fruit*. I place the bag back on the shelf, but don't bother closing the locker. "Thank you for your time, Mr. Wilkes."

"My pleasure. If there's anything else I can be of assistance with, please don't hesitate to call. Maggie's a good employee. She's never even called out sick once in all the time she's worked here." He shakes his head. "I just hope she's okay."

"We're going to do everything we can to find her," Mitchell assures him.

He gives us a nod and motions for us to return the way we came, but I have another idea.

"I'd like to leave through the door Maggie left through if you don't mind." I want to see the back employee parking lot since that's where Maggie was assaulted.

"Of course," Emit says. "By all means."

"Thank you again," Mitchell says as he follows me out the back, getting the door for me.

I step out slowly, the memory of Maggie being hit over the head as soon as she came out here replaying in my mind. I reach for my head again even though I know the pain isn't real. It just feels like it is.

"What are you sensing?" Mitchell asks.

"Nothing. She didn't even have time to be afraid because she was hit so quickly."

"So whoever took her knew she was on her way out here."

I nod. "It was the person who called her phone. I need you to trace the number I saw on her display." I take out my phone and text the number to him.

"As soon as I drop you off at your office, I'll head to the station." He runs a hand through his hair. "Who answers a call from an unknown number these days? Or did you get the sense she was expecting a call? I'd think if she was, the number would have been programmed in her phone and the call would have displayed a name instead."

"Agreed. She definitely didn't know who was calling."

Mitchell is looking around at the ground. "She must have dropped her phone, right?"

"I didn't see what happened after she was hit, but it's a good guess." I don't see how anyone would be able to hold onto a phone when they were knocked unconscious.

"There's nothing on the ground other than cigarette butts from the employees smoking out here."

I don't want to leave with this little to go on. "Let me see the list of employees." I hold my hand out to Mitchell. "Hopefully a name will jump out at me."

Mitchell pulls the folded paper from his back pocket and hands it to me.

I close my eyes and clear my mind before unfolding the paper and focusing on the names.

DRASTIC CRIMES CALL FOR DRASTIC INSIGHTS

One name practically jumps off the page at me. "Tanner Montgomery."

Mitchell moves next to me to see the paper for himself. "He's a butcher in the meat department. That seems almost too easy. A butcher being the bad guy."

"I'm not saying he took Maggie."

Mitchell takes a step back and eyes me. "Then why would his name stand out to you?"

"He has something to do with Maggie. I'm just not sure what it is. Let's go talk to Emit again. Maybe he can tell us more about Tanner." I start back inside.

Emit Wilkes is locking up his office. "Detectives, I was under the impression you'd left."

"We were on our way out, but one name on this employee list caught my attention." I turn the paper to him and tap Tanner's name. "What can you tell us about Tanner Montgomery?"

Emit frowns, and his throat constricts as he swallows hard. "Tanner's kind of a hothead. He's only worked here for about four months. Some of the female employees have filed complaints against him."

"Complaints for what?" Mitchell asks, his notepad and pen poised and ready.

"Crude comments mostly. He's never physically touched any of the female employees, but he says things about the way they're dressed and such. It's all written up in his personnel file. He's taking a sexual harassment seminar. It was a condition for him to remain employed here." Emit's chin drops. "You don't think he did something to Maggie, do you? I'd never forgive myself for keeping him on here if it turns out…" He inhales sharply, unable to finish the thought.

"Mr. Wilkes, has Mr. Montgomery ever seemed violent in nature?" I ask.

He shakes his head. "No. That's why I didn't fire him. He's just a stupid kid."

"Kid?" Mitchell asks, his brow raised.

"Well, he's twenty-seven."

A year younger than I am. I wonder if he sees me the same way.

"Ever since he started that seminar, I haven't gotten a single complaint about him. I swear. Not that I'm defending him. If he did something, you'll have my full cooperation."

"Thank you. We'll look into it." Mitchell puts his pen and notepad inside his jacket.

"Yes, thank you again for your time, Mr. Wilkes." I extend my hand to him.

"She's married. Leave her alone. You're already in enough trouble after Candice reported you."

"Relax. Maggie's not going to report me. All I did was tell her she had a nice rack. It was a compliment. She knows that."

Emit wags a finger at Tanner. "I'm not putting my neck out on the line for you again, Tanner."

"We both know Mom will make you stick up for me."

I let go of Emit's hand. "Tanner's your son." Emit's comment about Tanner being a "kid" makes more sense now.

"What?" Mitchell's gaze volleys between Emit and me.

"Stepson," Emit says. "How did you...?" He looks down at his hand. "I can't believe I fell for that."

"Are you saying you were trying to hide this from Piper?" Mitchell asks.

"I guess I didn't realize you could read people as well." Emit shoves his hands into his pockets. "As for hiding my relation to Tanner, I've tried to do that from the start. He's not exactly the model son. His father, my wife's first husband, was a convicted rapist."

"Was?" Mitchell asks.

Emit nods. "He's dead. He died in prison from testicular cancer."

I resist the urge to say he got what he deserved in the end. "I'm assuming you're afraid the apple doesn't fall far from the tree where Tanner is concerned." Apple. The apple in Maggie's lunch bag. Forbidden fruit. Is that what my senses were trying to tell me?

"My wife says he's nothing like his father. That Tanner's just all talk, but... With Maggie missing, I don't know what to think."

"We're going to need to speak to Tanner. Is he here now?" Mitchell asks.

"No. It's his day off."

"I assume he doesn't live at home anymore." Mitchell has his phone in hand.

"No. He rents an apartment on First Street. It's above the Italian restaurant."

Mitchell nods. "Then I think that's where we're headed next."

"Any chance you could keep me out of the conversation?" Emit asks. "My wife would kill me if she found out I said anything bad about Tanner."

"Don't worry, Mr. Wilkes. It was my vision that led me to Tanner." I turn on my heel and head for the back door.

Mitchell falls into step with me. "So, what are you thinking? Is Tanner our guy?"

"Could be. I'm not sure." I take one last look around the back parking lot. If only Maggie hadn't been hit so quickly. But that could mean the person who struck her was behind her the whole time, which would be possible if they work here, too. Like Tanner does.

We detour to my house so I can walk Jezebel, the golden retriever I acquired during our last case. After Jez's former owner was killed, she became my pet—though she's more like my therapy dog considering she's very attune to my visions and how to bring me out of the particularly bad ones.

She greets me with her usual barrage of kisses to my nose and cheeks. "Okay, okay. That's enough, Jez." I stand up and grab her leash from the kitchen counter.

"Want me to walk her?" Mitchell asks.

I know he's asking partly because he enjoys walking Jez and partly because he knows my landlord doesn't allow dogs and seeing me with Jez would put me at risk of being evicted for breaking the terms of my rental agreement.

"Sure," I say, handing him the leash. Though one of these days I really need to talk to Mr. Hall about Jez. Luckily for me, Dad is good friends with Theodore Hall and can hopefully pull some strings for me.

"Come on, Jez," Mitchell says, bending down to secure her leash.

"Be good for Mitchell," I tell her.

She gives a slight bob of her head as if in agreement.

Mitchell laughs. "You two are so in sync it's creepy."

"You should definitely be scared," I tell him. "You know I can read her and see exactly what you're doing when you're walking her. Like hitting on the blonde from the second floor."

His eyes widen. "I wasn't..." He huffs and walks out the door.

Seeing him squirm gives me way more pleasure than it

should. I grab my phone and call Dad to fill him in on my visions before asking what he's uncovered.

"I've checked all of Maggie's social media accounts. The last time she posted anywhere was at 8:37 Thursday night. She said she had a migraine and couldn't wait until her shift was over so she could go to bed."

"Is Tanner Montgomery one of her followers anywhere?" I ask.

"Let me check." He clicks some keys on his laptop, and I do my best to wait patiently. "Definite no on Instagram." More key clicks. "They aren't friends on Facebook." A few more clicks. "And Maggie's not on Twitter."

"Okay. Well, Mitchell and I are going to head to Tanner's apartment in a few. If that doesn't turn up any solid leads, we'll go talk to Maggie's husband."

"What's your gut telling you?" Dad asks.

I walk to the window and stare out at Mitchell and Jez walking along the sidewalk back to the apartment complex. "That the person who called her is the one who knocked her out. He was either waiting outside for her or followed her out of the back room."

"I assume Mitchell is running the number that called Maggie."

"Yeah, or at least he's going to." Mitchell had his phone to his ear as he walked back into the apartment building, so it's possible he called someone at the station to run the number.

"This is good. You're doing great, Piper."

"Want to meet us at Tanner's apartment?"

"No. You two go on ahead. I promised your mother I'd have lunch with her today."

"Okay, Dad. Enjoy, and give Mom a hug for me."

"Will do, pumpkin." He hangs up.

The door opens, and Jez comes bounding for me, making Mitchell drop the leash to avoid being dragged.

"Whoa. Easy, girl. Easy." I pocket my phone and bend down to pet her head, scratching behind her left ear, which is her favorite spot. "Did Mitchell hit on anyone out there?" I ask, pretending to read her.

"No, I didn't." He huffs. "Can we go now? This case isn't going to solve itself."

"You look way too eager to interrogate Tanner Montgomery."

Mitchell's expression becomes stone-cold serious. "You've read me before. You should know that while I've dated my share of women, I have the utmost respect for them. If this guy is anything like his father, then I want him behind bars for life."

I can't disagree with him, but my gut is telling me Tanner's name jumped out at me for another reason. And once again, I'm not sure what my abilities are trying to show me.

CHAPTER THREE

Mitchell's clutching the steering wheel so tightly he's leaving finger impressions in the leather.

"Maybe you should let me do the talking," I say.

"Yeah, as in introduce yourself and read the bastard on the spot. I want this case closed." He cuts the engine and gets out of the Explorer.

I meet him in front of the car. "It's not that simple. I saw Tanner getting yelled at for hitting on Maggie, but I don't think he was stupid enough to do something to her."

"Are you saying your vision was a dead end?"

"No. It means something."

He sighs, which is the most frustration he ever shows for my unclear visions. "Are you still trying to expand your abilities?"

I walk up to the door to the apartment building. "Always, but I'm not overdoing it if that's what you're thinking." He's seen how that can mess with my ability to interpret my visions. He must be convinced that's happening again now.

"Is there anything I can do to help?" He turns toward me, his hand on the door.

"I appreciate you wanting to, but I've got this." Having him there while I practice would only be a distraction.

"Is Jez helping?" He knows me too well.

"Yeah. Now enough about that. Let's go talk to Tanner so I can hopefully make sense of what my brain is trying to tell me."

He opens the door, holding it for me to enter first. Mitchell got Tanner's address while walking Jez, so we know he lives on the fourth floor in apartment 412. We take the elevator up, and as discussed, Mitchell stays one step behind me so I can take the lead on questioning Tanner. I raise my hand and knock three times.

Tanner comes to the door in workout clothes consisting of a sleeveless top and basketball shorts. He looks back and forth between us. "Can I help you?"

"Are you Tanner Montgomery?" I ask, even though I recognize him from my vision.

"That's me. Who's asking?" He looks me up and down, and I can feel Mitchell tense behind me.

"My name is Piper Ashwell." I extend my hand to Tanner, who looks hesitantly at me before shaking my hand.

"Come on, Maggie. Your husband would never find out. Just coffee. That's all I'm asking for."

"No. I told you, Tanner. I'm happily married. Now please leave me alone."

Tanner's hand is yanked from mine. When I open my eyes, Mitchell has Tanner by the front of his shirt.

"Stop." I pull Mitchell off him. "What the hell are you doing?"

"You didn't... He..." Mitchell's chest is heaving.

"I don't know who the hell you are, but I'm calling the cops," Tanner says, fixing his rumpled shirt.

"Don't bother. He's a police detective," I say, dipping my head in Mitchell's direction.

"I wish I'd videoed this. I could have your badge. You assaulted me for no reason."

"I stopped you from assaulting Piper," Mitchell says, keeping his body positioned between Tanner and me.

"What are you talking about?" My vision was seconds long at most. What could Tanner have tried to do to me in that time span? Mitchell's letting what he knows about Tanner's father cloud his judgment. "Maybe you should wait downstairs."

"Not a chance in hell." Mitchell's gaze is locked on Tanner.

I step to the side so I can see Tanner without the back of Mitchell's head blocking my view. "Mr. Montgomery, are you aware that your coworker Maggie Burns is missing?"

Tanner eyes Mitchell for a moment before returning his gaze to me. "Maggie? No. I haven't seen her since work on Thursday. I have the early shift on Fridays, and today is my day off."

"Did you happen to call her on Thursday night?" I ask.

"Call her? No. Like I said, we were both at work Thursday night. There would be no reason for me to call her. Besides, I don't have her number." He's the picture of calm, which means he's either innocent or a really good actor.

"Do you know if she had any plans for after work?"

He shrugs. "We didn't talk much."

More like Maggie didn't talk to him much. He definitely tried to talk to her.

"I think I remember her complaining about a headache."

Did she tell him that, or does he stalk her social media and saw her post? He doesn't follow her online, but that doesn't mean he doesn't visit her pages.

"How much did you two interact that night?"

"I work in the meat department, and she's in produce. We run into each other from time to time, but that's about it." He narrows his eyes at me. "How did you find out where I live?"

"We were checking out Maggie's personal belongings at the store, and I asked for a list of employees working on Thursday night. We're following up with as many people as we can track down to see if anyone has information that might be helpful in finding Maggie."

Mitchell gives me a look, most likely because I sound like him. I don't really want to let Tanner in on what it is I can do, though.

Tanner leans on the doorframe. "Well, sorry I can't be of any help. Do you have a card or number if I think of anything?" His question is directed at me, but Mitchell produces his card and holds it out to him.

"If you think of anything, you can call *me*," he says in a stern tone.

"I'm not interested in talking to you," Tanner responds before his gaze turns to me. "You, on the other hand, are welcome to stop by any time. Alone," he adds before closing the door.

"Man, I want to punch that guy right in the jaw." Mitchell turns away from the door, pocketing his card.

"Relax." I follow him back to the elevator. "I didn't see anything but him asking out Maggie. She turned him down, and it obviously wasn't the first time, but I didn't sense that she was afraid of him at all."

"I doubt you had time to sense much."

"No, I didn't, thanks to you. What was that about anyway? Why did you break my contact with him?"

He jabs the button to call the elevator and then stares up at the ceiling. "You didn't see the way he looked at you when you were holding his hand."

"First, I wasn't holding his hand. I was shaking it."

"Tell that to him. He was way too happy that you weren't letting go. He's just lucky I can't read minds or..."

"Or what? You'd risk your badge because some guy had a perverted thought about me? What the hell, Mitchell? I'm not helpless, you know. I can handle myself. Believe it or not, I've had guys have impure thoughts about me before, and I'm still here to tell the tale."

"This isn't a joke, Piper. Knowing his father was a..." The elevator arrives with three other people in it, cutting off our conversation for the time being.

Dad has dinner waiting for us when we arrive back at the office. "I figured neither one of you bothered to stop for food all day."

"You're a lifesaver," I say, slumping into my desk chair and digging into the chicken Caesar salad waiting for me.

"Any luck with Tanner?" Dad eyes me and then Mitchell, sensing the tension between us.

"I might have had more luck if this one"—I jab my plastic fork in Mitchell's direction—"hadn't lost it."

"What did you do?" Dad accuses him.

"I protected your daughter. Jeez, I'd think someone

would be happy about that." He shoves a huge chunk of chicken into his mouth.

"I don't need you to protect me. I'm not—" I stop myself from saying "your mom" because Dad doesn't know that Mitchell's mother was psychic. He doesn't know Mitchell's insane need to be around me stems from the fact that he couldn't save his mother. "I can take care of myself."

"She's right, you know. The more you try to intervene, the more she's going to fight you on it." Dad turns to me, his face beaming with pride.

"Fine. What's the plan from here? Do you suspect Tanner at all?" Mitchell reaches for his bottled water on my desk.

"I want to talk to Maggie's husband. See if Maggie complained about Tanner at home. I didn't feel like Tanner was a threat. He hit on Maggie, yes, but I don't think he ever took it beyond asking her out."

"Who asks out a married woman?" Mitchell shakes his head. "I really don't like that guy. Are you sure—?"

"I didn't get anything else from reading him. I think I'd know if he were the one who took Maggie." Sure, my visions have been unclear before, and in my last case one of the prime suspects was able to withhold information from me, but that was because I was taxing my abilities. I'm not doing that anymore. Trying to expand on what I can see has actually been getting a little easier. The other night, I sensed Jezebel was going to get sick after she ate some of my leftover Chinese food. I managed to get her outside before she threw up on any carpeting in my apartment.

Mitchell has the decency not to bring up times I've missed things. Instead, he eats in silence. In fact, he doesn't say another word for the rest of the evening.

DRASTIC CRIMES CALL FOR DRASTIC INSIGHTS

Sunday morning, Dad accompanies Mitchell and me to Maggie Burns's house to talk to her husband, Glen. They have a small place just outside of Weltunkin. It's not in a community, giving them some privacy since the road they live on is a back road and not well traveled by the looks of it. Dad parks in the gravel driveway and immediately checks to make sure none of the loose stones kicked up and scratched the underneath side of his BMW. Men and their cars. I'll never understand it.

The house is a brick bi-level with black shutters. I walk up the front steps and ring the doorbell. Mitchell is right behind me, but he's not very talkative today. I guess my comment about not needing his protection really got to him. He needs to get over it, though, or we won't be working many cases together after this one.

A man in his early thirties with blond hair answers the door. He's wearing workout clothes, and his upper lip and brow are glistening with beads of sweat. "Can I help you?"

"Mr. Burns," Dad says, "I'm Thomas Ashwell. We spoke on the phone this morning. This is my daughter, Piper, and Detective Brennan from the Weltunkin PD."

"Oh." Recognition washes over Glen's face. "Yes. Please come in. I thought I'd be able to finish my workout and get cleaned up before you arrived, but I must have lost track of time." He steps aside and motions for us to go up the stairs.

"He seems awfully calm for a guy whose wife is missing," Mitchell mumbles as we ascend the steps.

I can't deny he's got a point. Although it's possible Glen's workout was to burn off some pent-up emotions over his wife's disappearance, so I'm not going to accuse him of having his wife kidnapped just yet.

The inside of the house is much more impressive than the outside. Either Maggie or Glen—my senses are telling me it's Maggie—has a great eye for design. Everything has such contrast in bright white, pure black, and medium gray tones. A contemporary light fixture hangs from the ceiling in the entryway, and the floors are all hardwood.

"Your home is lovely," I say, turning toward the living room when I reach the top of the stairs.

Glen follows us up, wiping his brow with the bottom of his shirt. "Thank you. It's all Maggie." The warmth in his tone at the mention of his wife tells me he loves her.

"Mr. Burns, when was the last time you spoke to Maggie?" I ask, taking a seat on the edge of the black leather couch.

He takes a deep breath and holds onto the edge of the railing as if for support. "I think it was about a half hour before her shift was supposed to end." His last word is choked by a loud swallow.

"I understand it's difficult to talk about," I say. "Just please know we are doing everything we can to find out what happened to her Thursday night."

Glen nods. "She mentioned some sale on ground beef. She was going to talk to the butcher about getting a family pack for a party we were supposed to host yesterday."

Mitchell's already rigid form straightens further at the mention of the butcher. But I'm not convinced of anything. We already know Tanner was at work with Maggie that night. The fact that she spoke to him doesn't incriminate him in any way.

"Mr. Burns, were you aware that the butcher, Tanner Montgomery, was hitting on your wife?" Mitchell asks.

Glen's head whips in Mitchell's direction. "She told me he hits on a lot of the women who work there, but she never said he hits on her. I assumed her wedding ring deterred him."

"It would deter most, but Tanner—"

"What Detective Brennan is trying to say"—I stand up and glare at Mitchell before addressing Glen again—"is Mr. Montgomery has a habit of making inappropriate remarks to *all* the women he works with."

Glen's gaze remains on Mitchell. "Do you think this butcher—Tanner Montgomery—did something to my wife?" His fists are clenched at his sides.

"We don't know anything for sure yet, Mr. Burns," Dad says, being the voice of reason as usual.

Time to come clean. "Mr. Burns, I should tell you why I'm working on this case along with the Weltunkin PD. You see, I'm a private investigator, and I also happen to be psychic."

"Psychic?" He takes a step back as if I have some rare disease he might catch from being in my presence. "My wife's life is at stake, and I'm supposed to trust a *psychic* to save her?"

I'm surprised when Mitchell doesn't immediately come to my defense, but then again, I told him to stop trying to protect me. "Mr. Burns, I've solved many missing persons cases along with the Weltunkin PD. Now, you may not be a believer, but if you want your wife to be found before anything truly awful happens to her, I suggest you get me a personal belonging of hers so I can try to locate her."

"Personal belonging? What are you talking about? Why are you people here? Maggie is missing. That butcher probably took her and—"

"We've already questioned Mr. Montgomery, and we are fairly certain he had nothing to do with your wife's disappearance," Dad says, holding up a hand, warning Glen to calm down.

"Fairly certain?" Glen huffs and drags a hand through his hair. "Oh, well if you're *fairly certain*, then I'll be sure to sleep well tonight! We've got a psychic on the case. No need to worry about Maggie being hacked up into slabs of beef by some lunatic butcher. No! Not at all!"

"Enough," Mitchell says, positioning himself directly in front of Glen. "You might have your suspicions about Tanner and biased opinions about psychics, but you don't get to insult the woman who is your best shot at finding your wife. Are we clear on that?"

Dad eyes me, and I quickly look away.

"Mr. Burns, my abilities lie in reading objects. I've been able to find missing persons this way. If you'd just let me show you what I can do, I think you'll feel better about my involvement in the case."

Glen stares at me like I'm the headliner in a freak show. "Get the hell out of my house. All of you."

Mitchell takes a step toward him. "Don't—"

I grab the back of Mitchell's jacket and yank him away from Glen. "Let's go. The man wants us to leave, so we're going to leave."

Dad's already reaching for the front door. I push Mitchell out of the house behind him. But before leaving, I turn back to Glen. "Mr. Burns, I'm going to find your wife. And when I do, I'll look forward to your apology."

I slam the door so I don't have to listen to his retort.

CHAPTER FOUR

The roads are packed with the church crowd. Dad's trying to pretend it doesn't bother him, but his thumbs are tapping the steering wheel as we sit in the road while the traffic cop directs cars out of the church parking lot.

"Are all the men involved with this case complete assholes?" Mitchell asks from the front seat. He didn't offer to let me ride shotgun this time. Again most likely due to my outburst about his behavior around me.

"I've been insulted in worse ways by people much better than Glen Burns. Don't sweat it." I lean back and gaze out the window at the happy families getting into their cars. Sometimes, I think my life would be so much easier if I didn't have this gift. But then where would people like Maggie Burns be? I know where. In the hands of some psycho, which is where she is now since I haven't cracked this case yet.

Mitchell's phone rings, and he pulls it from inside his jacket to answer it. "Brennan. Uh-huh. Okay. Thanks, Wallace." He hangs up and turns to face me in the back seat. "One call was made from the number that called Maggie Thursday night. That's it."

"So it's a burner phone, and it's most likely already been discarded," I say, slumping back against the seat.

"That's my guess. It could imply this guy has done this before or that he's into some illegal activity."

"Dealing drugs?" Dad offers, edging the BMW up past the traffic cop since it's finally our turn in this long line of cars.

"Possibly." Mitchell is still staring at me like I'm going to have some big epiphany to crack the case wide open.

"A drug dealer who randomly decides to kidnap a woman who works at a grocery store?" I shake my head. "It doesn't add up."

"The drugs could be messing with his head," Dad says, pulling onto the road where our office is located.

No. That's not it, but he's right about one thing. Something was messing with someone's head. *My* head.

"God, I'm so stupid." I press my fingers to my temple. "I missed out on so many objects to read all because I let my headache make me careless. That and you opened the door for me." I reach forward and slap Mitchell on the side of his arm.

He grabs his arm as if I really belted him. "I'm being blamed for chivalry? Really?"

"I need to touch things to read them. That's how my abilities work. We've been through this, Mitchell. I didn't touch the back door because of you, and I didn't touch the locker combination because Emit Wilkes used his key to let us into it. I should have read both of those objects." This time I slam my open palm against my thigh.

"Are you finished taking your anger out on unsuspecting body parts?" Mitchell is practically facing backward in his seat now, like a parent turning around to reprimand a child in the back seat.

"I'm calling shotgun on all future rides together so you can't pull this"—I wave a finger in the air in front of him—"angry parent act on me. You're only two years older than I am, so stop treating me like I'm a child in comparison to you."

"A child?" His mouth hangs open for a second. "I've never treated you that way."

"Well..." Dad drags out the word, and the car makes an abrupt U-turn.

"What are you doing?" I ask, gripping the seat belt to keep from toppling across the seat.

"Going to the grocery store so you can read those two objects." He eyes me in the rearview mirror. "Unless you two would rather bicker some more. Though if that's the case, let me know and I'll drop you both off on the side of the road and continue on without you, because I'm sick of having to play referee all the time."

I cross my arms. "You were the one who made him your partner in the first place. We wouldn't be in this mess if you didn't."

Mitchell glares at me one last time before finally facing forward in his seat.

No one says another word until we arrive at Saves-A-Lot. We head directly for the back room to find Emit Wilkes, who doesn't seem all that surprised to see us again when we literally bump into him as he's exiting the back room.

"Detectives." Emit keeps his voice low so he doesn't attract the attention of the shoppers. "I had a feeling I'd be seeing you again. Come on back." He holds one of the double doors open for us.

I go first, heading immediately for Maggie's locker, but Emit calls after me, "In my office, please."

There are more workers around today being that it's a weekend, which I assume makes it a bigger shopping day for those who work during the week. I'm getting the vibe that Emit doesn't want his employees to think their work environment isn't safe.

We follow him into his office, and he shuts the door behind us. The room is small with only a desk and a single chair on each side. The only window is in the door itself. Anyone who is the least bit claustrophobic wouldn't survive for more than two minutes in this room.

"Mr. Wilkes, I'd really like to see Maggie's locker again, if you don't mind." I remain by the door.

He walks around the desk and takes a seat. "My stepson told me you stopped by to see him. He called out of work today. He's coming by later to pick up his paycheck, but he didn't want to be here in case you two showed up again." Emit's gaze falls on Dad. "We haven't been introduced. I'm Emit Wilkes, the store manager."

"Thomas Ashwell." Dad shakes Emit's hand.

Emit cocks his head in my direction. "A father-daughter team?"

I nod. "Tanner wasn't exactly happy we questioned him, but I don't think he's responsible for Maggie's disappearance. Feel free to convey that message to him."

Mitchell's chest rises and doesn't fall. He's still not convinced I'm right about Tanner.

Emit seems relieved though, his shoulders relaxing. "That's good to hear. But why do you need to see Maggie's locker again?"

"Mr. Wilkes, you're aware of what I can do. I believe I

can read more from Maggie's locker if I try opening it myself."

His brow furrows for a moment. "You can do that without knowing the combination?"

I tap the side of my head. "I can read Maggie opening the locker, and then I'll know the combination."

"I see." Emit stands up. "Will you give me a moment to clear the employee room? I'd rather you didn't have an audience while you work."

I'd rather not have an audience either. "Absolutely. I'd appreciate that."

He gives me a curt nod before walking out of the office, closing us inside once again.

Dad shoves his hands in his pockets. "If you ask me, he seems relieved to hear his stepson is innocent."

"We don't know he's innocent," Mitchell says, looking out the small window in the door.

"You might not believe me, but I know Tanner didn't do this." I'm really getting sick of the way he thinks he knows more about this case than I do.

"You didn't see the way he—"

Emit opens the door. "All clear, Detectives."

I don't even look at Mitchell as I push past him out the door. He tries to grab my arm but pulls away immediately. Emit walks me to Maggie's locker, his focus on me more intense than I'd like. He's very intrigued by what I can do.

I reach for the combination lock and close my eyes.

42-13-25. Maggie spins the dial and opens the locker.

Someone presses up against her from behind. His hands firmly gripping her arms and keeping her from pulling away or turning around.

"You smell so good. What shampoo do you use?"

Maggie's entire body tenses. "Please let go of me." Her

voice is calm. Really calm for someone who is married and being groped by another man.

The hands release her, and Tanner leans on her open locker door. "Come on. I just want to be friends. Just because you're married doesn't mean you can't be friends with another man, right?"

"We're coworkers, Tanner. That's it. If my husband knew you acted this way around me..."

Tanner leans closer. "I'm not afraid of your husband."

"I'm still not interested." Maggie's voice is stern so there's no mistaking she means what she says.

Tanner stands up straight. "Fine. It's your loss, though. Twenty bucks says your husband is bald in two years. You'd be better off with someone a little younger, like me. But suit yourself." He turns and walks away.

I let go of the locker and face Emit. "Your stepson certainly did try his best to get Maggie to go out with him." Out of the corner of my eye, I see Mitchell stiffen. "But she's tough. She was very stern with him, and in the end, he backed off. Maggie can definitely take care of herself." Which is good since she's in the hands of a kidnapper who could be a killer or rapist. She's going to need every ounce of strength and street smarts she has to survive if I don't find her soon.

"What else can I do?" Emit asks, and I don't need to read him to know he genuinely cares about Maggie's safety. "I was supposed to be here that night, but my wife called me. She got into a car accident, and I had to go pick her up."

So that's it. He feels guilty for not being here. If he'd been in his office, it might have prevented Maggie from being taken.

"Mr. Wilkes, you can't blame yourself. I promise I'm

DRASTIC CRIMES CALL FOR DRASTIC INSIGHTS

going to do everything I can to find Maggie and bring her home safely."

"Thank you."

I turn back to the locker. For some reason, the lunch bag draws my attention again.

"What is it?" Mitchell asks, his voice lacking the edge it had earlier.

"I'm not sure. Something is bothering me about this." I open the bag and look inside. "I'm just not sure why since it's only an apple."

"What?" Emit steps closer to me and peers into the bag. "That's strange. Maggie doesn't eat apples."

"She doesn't?" I furrow my brow.

"No. She hates them. I remember she picked them out of the fruit salad at our last staff party. I joked with her about it since she works in the produce department. It's like a butcher not liking meat, you know?"

"Why would she have one in her lunch then?" I ask.

"Maybe her husband packed her lunch and forgot she doesn't like them," Mitchell suggests.

No. My instincts are telling me that's not right. With my left hand, I reach into the bag and pull out the apple.

Mitchell gives me a look. "You're going to read the apple?"

"You have a better idea of finding out how it got in Maggie's lunch?" I challenge him.

He holds up his hands.

I take a deep breath and switch the apple to my right hand.

A gloved hand places the red apple into Maggie's lunch bag before closing it up and putting it back into the locker. Then the hand reaches for the picture of Maggie and her husband.

Forbidden fruit.

"Can I tempt you, Maggie?"

A ringing breaks me out of the vision. I open my eyes to see Mitchell on the phone. "Thanks for letting me know. We'll be right there." He hangs up the phone and locks his eyes on me. "Glen Burns is down at the station. He was just booked for assaulting Tanner Montgomery."

CHAPTER FIVE

Emit doesn't look all that concerned for his stepson. He seems more worried that his wife will be angry with him for allowing Tanner to get caught up in this mess. As if it's Emit's fault. He opts to go home to his wife while we head to the station.

Mitchell calls Marcia on the way and orders us some muffins and coffee to go. The way those two are getting along lately makes me wonder what's going on between them. Are they secretly dating behind my back? I'd think I'd sense that from one of them. Dad pulls up to Marcia's Nook next to my office, and I jump out before Mitchell can, yelling, "Be right back," as I slam the door of the BMW behind me. I rush inside Marcia's Nook, which is filled with people. Apparently, there's an author book signing today, and the kids and parents came out in droves to get autographed books.

I walk up to the counter, where the line is much longer than I have time to wait for. Why didn't Marcia tell Mitchell she was this busy when he called to order food? Marcia eyes me and motions to a teenage boy behind the counter with her. He must be a new employee. Most days, Marcia works alone since the store doesn't get that busy. It's sad how few people go to physical bookstores anymore. But weekends can get hectic, so she usually has help.

"Piper," Marcia says, grabbing a box from behind the counter. As she approaches, I see there is a drink carrier with three large coffees and a large white pastry bag. "I packed extra. I have a feeling none of you has eaten anything today. How you all survive is beyond me." She looks up and down my too-thin frame. My lack of curves doesn't come from not eating, though. My figure is due to a fast metabolism and genetics.

"Thanks, Marcia. You're a lifesaver." I feel like I'm constantly telling her that, but it bears repeating. "Could you possibly put it on my tab? We have to get down to the station, and that line is really long."

"Of course. No worries. Besides, I think all the tips Detective Brennan has left me covers all this and then some."

"I'm going to pay you for all of this. Those tips are yours, and they are well earned." I take the box from her and nod in the direction of the counter. "Looks like your new hire is struggling with the register. You better go. Thank you again."

"Anytime, hon." She smiles and rushes off to help her employee.

I weave through little kids running around and their parents chasing after them, making my way to the door. I let out a sigh when the door opens and freedom is in my sights.

"I take it you don't like kids," Mitchell says, and I realize he's the one who opened the door.

"They're fine. I just don't plan on having any of my own."

DRASTIC CRIMES CALL FOR DRASTIC INSIGHTS

"I hear you," he says, taking the box from my hands. He waves over my head, presumably at Marcia, before letting the door close behind me.

"What's going on with you two?" I ask as we walk back to Dad's car.

"What do you mean?"

"Are you seeing her?"

He gives me a look that's nothing short of "You've got to be kidding." "When would I have time to go out on a date? I spend all my time with you." He bumps his arm into mine.

I'm not sure why the prospect of Mitchell dating Marcia would bother me this much. After all, I did offer to set them up weeks ago. But now...it's weird. She's my only real friend, and Mitchell is my... Damn it. He's my partner. I guess I have to stop fighting that and just admit it.

"Green is a good color on you," Mitchell says, stopping to look at me before opening the car door.

I look down at my white shirt. "I'm not wearing green."

He smirks. "One day, you'll admit you're attracted to me and can't bear the thought of me with another woman."

"Oh, green. I get it now. I *am* feeling rather queasy. Hopefully, whatever Marcia packed in here for us will settle my stomach before we have to interrogate Glen Burns." I push him aside and get in the front passenger seat.

Mitchell laughs as he gets in the car. "Well played, Piper."

"Do I even want to know?" Dad asks, giving us both exasperated looks.

"No," Mitchell and I say in unison.

By the time we reach the station, we've each inhaled a muffin—or two in Mitchell's case—and downed our coffee. We're directed to the interrogation room where Glen is waiting for us.

Glen Burns is slumped in the chair on the opposite side of the table, but he sits up straight when he sees us. "Did you arrest him? He took my wife. I know he did. That sick pervert. He has my Maggie."

Mitchell leans close to my ear and whispers, "Is he being sincere or putting on a show for us?"

Oddly enough, I'm sensing a little of both. "Let's find out," I say before walking over to take the seat opposite Glen. "Mr. Burns, what makes you so sure Mr. Montgomery is responsible for Maggie's disappearance? You told us you weren't even aware of his interactions with your wife, so how can you jump to the conclusion that he's guilty in some way?"

He looks past me to Dad and Mitchell. "I'm not talking to some quack who says she's psychic. If you want to get anything out of me, she leaves first." He crosses his arms and leans back in his chair, looking like a stubborn five-year-old who didn't get his way.

"I'd watch—"

I hold up my hand to stop Mitchell. Once I'm satisfied he'll listen, I lean forward, placing my arms on the table between Glen and me. "Mr. Burns, are you aware your wife doesn't eat apples?"

Glen laughs. "That's the best you've got? Do you really think you'll convince me you're 'psychic'"—he makes air quotes—"by telling me Maggie doesn't like apples? I'm not an idiot." He resumes his former position with his arms crossed.

"I actually learned that fact from Maggie's boss. I did, however, see your wife being hit on by Tanner Montgomery, who didn't seem threatened at all by you. I also saw someone put an apple in her lunch bag. Now tell me, why

DRASTIC CRIMES CALL FOR DRASTIC INSIGHTS

would someone do that when Maggie doesn't even like apples?"

He leans forward and narrows his eyes at me. "Why don't you tell me, Ms. Psychic? You had the so-called vision. Who did you see?"

Ignoring his mockery, I ask, "Do you own black gloves?"

"I don't wear gloves unless they're weightlifting gloves." He scoffs and looks up at the ceiling as if completely bored with my questioning.

It definitely wasn't weightlifting gloves in my vision. I want more than anything to grab his hand and read him. Then I'd find out what I need to know and I wouldn't have to listen to him anymore. Win, win. But I can't do it against his will. He's the type to press charges, and he's already made his feelings about me and my abilities crystal-clear.

"Do you know of anyone at Saves-A-Lot who might have been arguing with Maggie? A coworker perhaps?"

"She doesn't really talk about work much. Look, I said I wasn't talking to you. I've entertained your little game for long enough, but I'm done now."

I stand up, but then I remember something. "Mr. Burns, when we showed up at your house, you weren't wearing a wedding ring."

"Yeah, because I was working out. I never wear it when I work out. It could get damaged by the weight bars." He rolls his eyes like I'm a complete moron, but there's something else there. He's avoiding my gaze because he's hiding something.

"When *do* you wear it?" Not now because his personal belongings were taken when they arrested him. But if he never wears it, there could be a reason.

"Like I said, I'm done talking to you." He waves his hand in my direction. "Get out of here. Go!"

I move closer to him, and Mitchell falls in step with me, obviously not trusting Glen to remain calm when I'm pressing him like this. "You don't wear it at work, do you? You only wear it at home or when you're out with Maggie." I'm guessing, but his body language is telling me I'm right. I take a few deep breaths, willing my senses to pick up on something. Then I take a big leap. "How long have you been having an affair?"

Mitchell inhales sharply at my side.

"How dare you?" Glen stands up and turns away from me, and my senses are ringing. I'm dead-on about the affair.

"You weren't wearing your ring when you attacked Tanner Montgomery, were you?" I ask, stepping toward him again.

"Now I know you're guessing. My ring was taken along with my other things." He turns to me with a smile on his face, thinking he's got me, but he played right into my plan.

I return his smile. "Detective Brennan, would you be so kind as to retrieve Mr. Burns's ring for me? I'd like to personally show him what I can do."

"It would be my pleasure," Mitchell says.

"What are you going to do?" Glen's gaze volleys between me and Mitchell. "Wait. What's going on?"

I hear the click of the door as it closes behind Mitchell, and I sit down in the chair, pretending to inspect my nails, which are chipped and in dire need of some TLC.

"Someone tell me what's going on!" Glen shouts.

"I was thinking of checking out that new Mexican place on Main Street for dinner. You up for that, Dad?" I ask, completely ignoring Glen's outburst.

"Your mother's been asking to go there. I could call her right now," Dad plays along, removing his phone from inside his jacket.

Glen is losing it more by the second. His hands are gripping the sides of his blond hair.

When Mitchell returns with Glen's wedding ring, Glen lunges for him, which is the worst thing he could possibly do. Mitchell has him pinned on the ground in seconds.

"Here, let me hold that for you," I say, reaching for the wedding ring with my left hand. Mitchell hands it over. "Mr. Burns, you might feel differently about my abilities in a moment." He stares up at me as I transfer the ring to my right hand.

Glen rolls over and checks the time on his phone. "Maggie will be home soon. You need to leave." He turns back to the naked blonde in his bed.

She pouts. "So soon? I feel like I just got here."

"Yeah, well now it's time to go. You know the deal. Maggie can't know about this."

The woman gets out of the bed and starts redressing. "I don't get you at all. If you love your wife so much, what are you doing with me?"

Glen props his head on his hand, supporting the weight with his bent elbow. "Maggie's good for me, but she's also a little too proper to meet all my needs. You on the other hand..." His smile says what his sentence left off.

I switch the ring to my left hand, not wanting to see any more. I hate having visions that involve intimate moments between people. They always tell me much more than I need or, more accurately, *want* to know. "So you love your wife, but the blonde woman you're sleeping with fulfills your freaky desires in the bedroom. The bedroom you share with your wife, I might add." I hand the ring to Dad, not wanting to touch anything that belongs to Glen Burns. "I'm done here." I start for the door but turn back to see Mitchell has Glen on his feet again. I glare at Glen. "Were you worried Maggie was having an affair with Tanner? Did you think she was doing all the things with him that she wouldn't do with you? Because I don't think you really believe Tanner took her."

Glen doesn't need to confirm my suspicions. My senses are tingling with affirmation.

"Well, you can rest easy. Your wife isn't the lowlife you are. She was upholding her end of your marriage vows. She turned Tanner down. You, on the other hand, are disgusting, Mr. Burns. And you should know that when I find your wife, I plan to share this information with her."

"No!" Glen yells. "Stop! You don't know anything!"

I let the door close behind me. Just like I allowed the door to close on the possibility of ever being in a relationship a long time ago.

CHAPTER SIX

Back at the office, I'm ready to pack it in and call it a day. Men like Glen Burns make me feel better about my decision to never get involved with anyone. Maggie probably had no idea he was having an affair. Yet the prospect of her doing the same thing sent Glen into a jealous rampage. One good thing to come from interrogating Glen was that I now know neither he nor Tanner is responsible for what happened to Maggie. But the bad part is I'm no closer to solving this case than when I first started.

"See you tomorrow, pumpkin. Get some rest," Dad says from the front seat of his BMW.

I give him a small nod and remove my car keys from my purse. Much to my dismay, Mitchell follows me to my Mazda 6. "I'm too tired for this," I say, opening the driver's side door and cocking my head at him.

"What did I do now? I was just going to ask if you wanted me to stop by with some dinner so we can hash out this case." He shoves his hands into his pants pockets and shrugs awkwardly.

"There's nothing to hash out. We have exactly nothing."

I know he's only trying to help, but when my visions don't show me what I need them too, it makes me irritable and poor company. Having Mitchell help me try to make sense of them will only aggravate me more. "Stop looking at me like I just took away your favorite chew toy." I get in the car and close the door, lowering the window.

"So I'm a dog now?" He steps forward and places his hands on the roof of the car as he leans down toward the window. "Why do you always feel the need to put me in my place? Is it really that difficult for you to let someone in?"

He knows I have exactly one friend, Marcia. My social awkwardness shouldn't come as a surprise to him anymore. "Why do you insist on pushing me? The fact that I willingly work with you should show you I'm trying to open up as much as I can, but you have no idea..." I stop when his face falls. "Okay, you have some idea, but I think that makes it worse, Mitchell. When you're around me, your emotions go from one extreme to the other."

"Oh, and yours don't?" He stands up straight and crosses his arms, looking out at the empty parking lot over the roof of my car. "We're a lot more alike than you're willing to admit. Maybe that's the real problem. You see in me the things about yourself that you..."

I know he was going to say "don't like." "I don't dislike you, Mitchell. And I don't dislike myself either. We are our jobs. I'm fine with that. It's the other part. The part where you think being partners means being friends and talking on a personal level. I don't do feelings well."

He lowers his gaze to meet mine. "Neither do I. Why do you think I live in a town where I can only afford a small condo? Why do you think I chose a profession where you have to keep your feelings out of what you do? Why do you think I date—?"

"Random women who mean nothing to you," I finish for him. I get it, but it doesn't make it any better.

"I told you I haven't dated anyone for a while now."

"I know."

"For the record, I'd never date Marcia. She deserves so much better than I could ever give her."

I can read the energy pulsing off of him right now. He doesn't think he's worthy of being with anyone. He thinks he's too damaged. God, he's right. We are too damn alike.

"Wonton soup," I say.

"What?" His brow furrows.

"Bring some wonton soup. It's chilly this evening. Oh, and pick up some apples. I have an idea. Now, I have to get home and walk Jez before she ruins the carpeting in my apartment." I start the car, and Mitchell takes a step back so I can pull out of my parking spot. "And don't dawdle. I don't want to be up too late," I call out the window.

After walking Jez and taking a quick shower, I settle on the couch in my comfy PJs, which are actually yoga pants and a sweatshirt I've had since college. Mitchell knocks on the door seconds after I get comfortable.

"It's open," I yell, and Jez gives a bark as if to say the same. I pet her head. When Mitchell walks in, Jez jumps down off the couch and rushes over to greet him. I'm glad Jez feels so at home here. I worried about how she'd handle the transition to being my dog.

"How's my favorite girl?" Mitchell asks Jez, bending down to accept a kiss across his face. "I brought you something, too."

"You did?" I ask, shifting on the couch so I'm facing the kitchen where Mitchell is already getting bowls for us.

He reaches into his coat pocket and pulls out a large dog biscuit. "Sit." Jez promptly sits, her tail swishing back and forth across the floor as she tries to control her excitement over the bone in Mitchell's hand. Mitchell holds out his free hand. "Paw." Jez slaps her paw onto his open palm. "Good girl." He gives her the bone, which she immediately digs into.

"So tell me what the apples are for," Mitchell says, ladling the wonton soup into two bowls.

"What do you think, Detective?" I snap my fingers in the air and motion for him to throw an apple to me.

He stops what he's doing and tosses an apple my way. "How can you read an apple that the kidnapper never even touched?"

"It's kind of like how I recall visions by mimicking sounds or something else from the vision. I need to know if I missed anything when I saw the gloved hand place the apple in Maggie's lunch bag."

"What makes you think you missed something?" Mitchell carries the bowls of soup to the coffee table.

"I'm not sure I did, but since we have nothing else to go on, I figure it can't hurt to try this, right?"

Mitchell heads back to the kitchen and retrieves the Chinese noodles. "You should eat first."

I wave my free hand in the air. "I'll need my strength more after the vision than before it." I turn the apple over in my left hand. It's bigger than the apple I found in Maggie's lunch, but it will have to do. I close my eyes and try to block out the feel of Mitchell's gaze on me.

A gloved hand places the red apple into Maggie's lunch bag before closing it up and putting it back into the locker. Then the hand reaches for the picture of Maggie and her husband.

Forbidden fruit. The gloved finger is almost petting Maggie's hand.

"Can I tempt you, Maggie?"

The vision ends. As soon as I open my eyes, I can tell Mitchell is dying to ask what I saw. I give him credit for not pushing me in times like this, though. He even takes a spoonful of the steaming soup while he waits for me. Jez jumps up on the couch and places her head in my lap. I swear she senses when I'm using my abilities, and she always seeks to comfort me.

"I'm okay, Jez." I put the apple down on the table and stroke the top of her head. "I noticed one more thing," I tell Mitchell. "The gloved hand was actually focused on Maggie's hand in the picture."

"Her hand? Why?"

"Forbidden fruit. Maggie is the forbidden fruit. It was her left hand. I think the gloved hand was petting the wedding band on Maggie's ring finger."

"So the kidnapper left the apple because it's a symbol for forbidden fruit? We have a kidnapper who enjoys symbolism?" Mitchell places his spoon back in the bowl. "But who else but you would even pick up on this? It doesn't make sense."

"Unless that's part of the fun for this guy. He's only leaving clues he thinks no one will figure out."

"Guy? You're sure the kidnapper is male?" He turns on the couch cushion and motions for Jezebel to come to him, most likely because he wants me to eat my soup now that the vision is out of the way.

"I am. And he somehow had access to the employee room at Saves-A-Lot." I sit forward and take a spoonful of soup.

"So it's an employee."

No. I can sense that's wrong. "He doesn't work there."

"Then how did he get in there? Is he related to a

worker? Or a friend maybe? Someone who was giving a ride to an employee?" Mitchell is thinking aloud in hopes one of his suggestions will trigger my senses as truth. None do, though.

I shake my head and eat the rest of my soup, wondering how I'm ever going to solve this case.

―――

Marcia's Nook isn't as crowded Monday morning. Most people are getting ready for school or work, not shopping for books, which is why I'm here now. I hate crowds. I search the mystery section, looking specifically for books where characters have been kidnapped in the hope that something I read will spur an idea or some clue as to who the mystery forbidden fruit giver is.

"You're taking longer than usual to pick a book," Marcia says. "Everything okay?"

I huff. "Tough case. I'm looking for something specific, but like with the case, I can't seem to find it."

"Maybe it's not good that you're always in work mode. You need time to relax, Piper. You're putting too much pressure on yourself." She turns around to the shelf behind us. "How about a romantic comedy? You know, something light."

"Romance isn't really my thing." I simply can't relate to the characters at all. And for some reason, reading about happy couples doing "happy couple" things is almost as bad as accidentally seeing it in a vision. I try to avoid it at all costs.

"Okay, then what about fantasy or historical fiction? Sci-fi maybe?"

"Maybe I should just watch TV."

DRASTIC CRIMES CALL FOR DRASTIC INSIGHTS

Marcia laughs. "When do you ever put that thing on unless Mitchell or your dad is at your apartment?"

How does she know Mitchell watches TV at my place? He said they weren't dating, but was he lying to me?

"Did Mitchell tell you that?" I place yet another book that isn't what I'm looking for back on the shelf and turn to Marcia.

She cocks her head at me. "He told me you've never seen *Matlock* or *Murder She Wrote* despite them always being replayed late a night when we're both sure you're still awake."

"I didn't realize you two talked."

"Only ever about you. I'm starting to think you're his favorite topic of conversation." Her tone softens. "He cares about you, you know. He worries that I'm your only friend. You really should socialize with more than three people, Piper. You never know what you could be missing out on."

"Why do I get the feeling you mean *who* I might be missing out on?"

She gives a guilty shrug.

"I'm suited for the single life. I'm okay with that. And with my line of work, I can't trust a lot of people to know too much about me." The look of pity that washes over her face is too much to bear. I hold up my hand before she can tell me how awful my life is. "I'm really okay with it. I've been this way since my abilities came on when I was twelve. I don't know any other way of living, so I can't miss what I've never had."

She places her hand on my arm. "Then at least give Detective Brennan a real chance at being your friend. You're a great person, Piper. And underneath that tough guy exterior, Detective Brennan is a great person, too."

I don't make empty promises, so I just smile. "I think I

need an extra large toasted almond today and an apple turnover."

She frowns, but then she clears her throat and says, "Coming right up."

I follow her to the bakery counter, giving up on finding a new book to read.

The bell over the door dings as I'm paying.

"Piper, I knew I'd find you here." Mitchell's tone tells me he has news, and it isn't good.

"What happened?" I ask, turning toward him with my coffee and pastry bag.

"There's been another kidnapping."

CHAPTER SEVEN

Back at my office, I take a seat at my desk, dumping my purse in the bottom drawer. I take a healthy sip of hot coffee and say good morning to Dad before gesturing to Mitchell. "Lay it on me."

"Carmen Ramon didn't show up for work this morning. She's a secretary in an office building on Main Street. Apparently, there was a big meeting this morning, and Carmen was going to help her boss make a presentation to the higher-ups. She was supposed to be there at 6:00 a.m. When she was late, her boss called her cell. She didn't answer, so he asked one of her coworkers if they'd heard from Carmen. The coworker was directed to go to Carmen's home since she's friends with Carmen. Carmen's car is in the driveway, but Carmen wasn't home." Mitchell blurts it all out, leaning forward with his arms resting on his knees.

"How old is she?" Dad asks, his pen and pad out.

"Forty-five, but in the picture I saw of her, she looks more like she's in her early thirties. Pretty woman."

"Like Maggie," I say.

Mitchell nods. "Yeah, well attractive women are often the prey of kidnappers."

"No." My senses are saying there's more to this. "I think Carmen was kidnapped like Maggie, meaning by the same person."

"You think the two cases are related?" Dad asks.

"I know it."

Mitchell gets to his feet. "Want to come with me to talk to Carmen's coworker then? She's going to meet me at Carmen's house so I can look around. I'd love to have your help."

Twenty minutes later, we're parked behind Carmen's car in the driveway. Without knowing why, I walk right up to her car. My senses are leading me, and I'm not about to stop to question them. Mitchell knows better than to interrupt me in moment's like this. I reach for the driver's side door handle and tug. To my surprise, the door isn't locked. I pull it wide open and am immediately bombarded with a foul odor.

"What is that smell?" Mitchell asks, covering his nose. "It's sweet but sour and rotten smelling at the same time."

I peer into the car. In the middle console where the cup holder is located sits a red fruit. I reach for it. "This. I'm willing to bet this pomegranate is rotten inside. It's been left in the car for who knows how long."

"But that would mean Carmen has been gone for a while, too," Mitchell says.

"When was the last time anyone saw her?"

He shrugs. "She lives alone. Let's go talk to her friend. She should be inside."

I take the pomegranate up to the front door of the colonial, not willing to part with it just yet. Thankfully, the odor isn't as strong out in the open. "Big house for someone who lives alone," I say as Mitchell rings the doorbell.

"The property is in Carmen's parents' names. I think she lived with them. My guess is they either retired and gave her the house, or they aren't alive anymore and she inherited the house."

A woman in her forties opens the red front door. "Detective Brennan?" she asks.

"Yes, I'm Detective Mitchell Brennan, and this is my partner, Piper Ashwell. She's a private investigator assisting me with this case."

The woman nods in my direction. "Won't you both please come in?" She steps aside to let us pass.

The interior of the house is nice but seriously dated. I'm going with Carmen's parents were the last to decorate it. We follow the woman to the living room off to the left of the entryway.

"Can I get either of you something to drink? I haven't looked in the refrigerator, but I'm sure Carmen has something in there." She looks frazzled. "Oh, where are my manners? Ms. Ashwell, I'm Colleen McDonald. I work with Carmen, and we also happen to be best friends."

She extends her hand, and I don't attempt to read her. Instead, I focus on not allowing myself to read her. The worry she's feeling about her friend's safety tells me all I need to know about her.

"Pleasure to meet you, Colleen. And Detective Brennan and I don't need anything to drink. We just have a few questions for you, and then we'll be on our way."

Colleen gestures to the oversized couch, and Mitchell and I sit down. She takes a seat in the matching armchair.

Mitchell takes out his phone. "Do you mind if I record our conversation?"

"Not at all. Go right ahead. I just want Carmen found. I still can't believe she's missing. It's surreal." She's practically wringing her hands in her lap.

"I assure you we will do everything we can to find her and bring her home safely as quickly as possible," I say.

"Thank you." Colleen swallows hard.

"Can you tell us the last time you spoke with Carmen?" I ask.

"I think it was Friday night. We had a late meeting at work. There was this big presentation set for today, and our boss was being such a pain in the ass about it." She covers her mouth, and her gaze falls on the phone in Mitchell's hand. "You won't play this recording for anyone else, will you?"

"The only person who might hear it is my father, who works with me at my PI agency," I say.

"Oh, okay, good. My boss is a dick, but I need my job. Carmen lucked out with this place. It was her parents. They left it to her in their will. It's paid off, so that's one less living expense Carmen has to worry about. I live in a tiny apartment that costs almost as much as my college tuition." She laughs. "The things we do to say we live in a wealthy area, am I right?"

The pomegranate in my left hand feels unusually warm, making me wonder if it's been inside the car since Carmen returned from work on Friday night. "By any chance, do you remember if Carmen brought this pomegranate to work on Friday?"

"Pomegranate?" Colleen sits forward in her chair. "I've never seen Carmen eat one. She hates anything with seeds."

Another fruit clue? Is this really possible? And if so, why a pomegranate this time instead of an apple?

"Is that what I'm smelling?" Colleen asks, her nose wrinkling.

"How did Carmen seem when you last spoke to her?" Mitchell asks, getting back on topic.

"Annoyed. Mr. Sherman—that's our boss—was in such a foul mood. He treats his secretaries like trash. And yes, he has several because God forbid the man does any menial work himself." She puts her hand on her chest in mock horror.

"So you didn't talk to her at all over the weekend?" I ask.

"No. I had a christening to go to for my nephew. We had to fly to Atlanta for the weekend. I just got back late last night." Her brows pull together. "Now that I think about it, it is weird that I didn't hear from Carmen all weekend. Usually when I have family obligations, she sends me texts to help me get through them. My husband's side of the family can be more than a little trying at times."

That could mean Carmen was abducted any time after she got home from work on Friday night.

"Do you know if she happened to have a date this weekend?" Mitchell asks.

"Not that I knew of. She usually tells me when she's seeing someone new. But like I said, work last week was intense. We didn't have much free time to talk. We were both exhausted each night by the time we got home. I slept on the plane ride Saturday morning, and I probably would have slept through the christening, too, if my husband would have let me." She gives a small chuckle, but it's sad. "When Carmen didn't show up this morning, I was convinced she'd overslept. Mr. Sherman told me to come here since he had to cancel his meeting. I'm sure he wanted me to catch her slacking off so he could fire her. As if I'd ever rat her out that way. The man is an idiot." She reaches out with her hand. "You're sure he'll never hear this recording?"

"You have nothing to worry about," Mitchell tells her.

"Mrs. McDonald, is there anything else you can think of that might help us find Carmen sooner?" I only add "sooner" to keep her from breaking because her emotions are all over the place right now.

"Actually, yes. Carmen usually gets up early to go for a morning run before work. Since we were supposed to be at the office by 6:00 a.m., I can't be sure if she did or not, but there's a trail at the end of the road. It leads to a park. That's where Carmen runs. It's possible something happened to her on her morning run." Colleen rubs her arms as if trying to hug herself.

"Thank you, Mrs. McDonald. You've been very helpful," Mitchell says, standing up.

I stand as well, and after we both shake Colleen's hand and Mitchell gives her his card, we head back outside.

"Want to check out that trail?" he asks me as we get into his Explorer.

"Definitely." I click my seat belt and hold up the pomegranate. "But first, it's time to read this. If Carmen doesn't eat seeds, she'd never touch a pomegranate, which means our kidnapper left it."

"This is the strangest case. I mean, you're reading fruit." He backs out of the driveway and turns toward the end of the road where the trail is.

I clear my mind and transfer the fruit to my other hand.

The gloved hand places the pomegranate in the middle console.

"Aged forbidden fruit." He laughs at his own joke. "Still so tempting."

DRASTIC CRIMES CALL FOR DRASTIC INSIGHTS

When nothing else comes to me, I open my eyes. Mitchell is parked and staring at me.

"Same guy. Same message. Except I'm guessing he's younger than Carmen because he referred to the fruit—that we also know symbolizes these women—as 'aged forbidden fruit.'"

Mitchell nods. "That definitely does make it seem like he's younger than she is. Okay, so we're looking for a male under the age of forty-five, who wears gloves."

"Easy peasy, right?" I get out of the Explorer and walk right over to the garbage can at the entrance to the trail.

"Wait," Mitchell says, coming after me. "There might be fingerprints on that."

"There are. Mine. And the person who stocks the fruit in the produce aisle. The kidnapper wore gloves, though. He didn't get a single print on this fruit." I toss it into the garbage can.

"Hey, why didn't you try to read anything of Carmen's while we were at the house?"

"I didn't get the feeling anything happened to her there." I look at the trail entrance. "This seems more likely, which means the kidnapper knew Carmen's routine. He could have waited for her somewhere on the trail and taken her without anyone else seeing."

Mitchell gestures for me to go ahead. "Then let's go look for signs of a struggle."

The problem is, Carmen could have been taken on Saturday morning. A well used trail wouldn't show much after a few days. And that means I have to rely on my senses to pick up on something.

The only people on the trail, given that it's a Monday morning, are mothers pushing strollers and elderly people trying to get some exercise. Before long, we find ourselves trapped behind two old ladies who are walking so slowly they make sloths look like sprinters.

"Pardon me," Mitchell says, trying to get their attention.

The woman in front of him turns around and nearly falls in the process. I'm not sure either of these women should be out here on their own like this. Mitchell catches her and doesn't let go until she's steady on her feet again. "Ladies, this path is a little uneven. Are you sure this is where you want to get your morning exercise?"

The woman pats his cheek. "Such a handsome young man. Shirley, isn't he handsome?"

"Peg, I think he's spoken for." Shirley hitches her thumb in my direction.

I wave off the comment. "Oh, no, Peg. He's not spoken for at all. Please be my guest."

Mitchell widens his eyes at me as Peg squeezes his bicep.

"So strong, too. I think he might be right about this trail. Perhaps he can escort two eighty-five-year-*young* women back to their house."

I stifle a laugh.

"You live around here?" Mitchell asks.

Peg smacks his arm playfully. "Fresh little thing, trying to find out where we live."

Mitchell eyes me, silently pleading for help.

"You go on ahead, Mitchell. You can catch up with me when you're finished."

"I would've guessed you had a strong sounding name like Mitchell." Peg's laying it on thick, and I'm loving every second of it.

"Mitchell, be a dear and offer Peg and Shirley each an arm to see them safely home. And don't you go spending too much time at their place. We do have work to do, you know." I wag a finger at him and quickly turn around before I burst out laughing.

With how slowly Peg and Shirley move, I know it will be a little while before Mitchell returns. I can't afford to waste time, no matter how funny Mitchell's current predicament is, so I start along the trail again. I make it all the way to the park without finding so much as a mark on the trail from a sneaker dragging across the dirt and rocks. Maybe Mitchell was right about me reading something of Carmen's back at the house. I just really felt like this trail had answers for me. How could I be so wrong?

I sit down on a bench at the end of the trail and look up at the sky. It's a beautiful day, despite the slight bite in the crisp air. I've always loved fall weather. It smells so fresh. I breathe deeply and place my hands beside me on the bench.

Carmen is seated on the bench, breathing heavily after her run. Her chest rises and falls in quick succession. She lifts the water bottle in her left hand and takes a large gulp. Her breathing becomes even heavier after she swallows.

"New best time," she thinks to herself.

She starts to smile when the gloved hand reaches around her from behind. The sweet smell of chloroform hits her nostrils as a white cloth is brought over her nose and mouth.

My head lolls back against the bench as my world goes completely dark.

CHAPTER EIGHT

"Piper." Mitchell's panicked voice infiltrates my head, which feels like it's pounding with every beat of my heart.

"Shh. Not so loud." I press my hand to the top of my head and open my eyes to find I'm in Mitchell's arms.

"You know, you don't have to fake an injury every time you want a hug. You could just ask." He offers a weak smile, but it's clear he's worried about what I experienced in my vision.

I sit up with his help. "Carmen was attacked right here on this bench." I slowly turn around to face the bushes behind the bench. "The kidnapper was waiting in that bush. He knocked her out with chloroform."

"That explains your symptoms. You're literally swaying even though you're sitting down."

I know the dizziness I'm feeling isn't real, but damn it if it doesn't seem real to me.

Mitchell looks around the park. "There's a hot dog vendor. Let me get you something to eat. It might help." He gets up but then second-guesses himself. "Will you be okay on your own for a second?"

I try to nod, but the dizziness takes over.

Mitchell kneels in front of me. "Easy. We'll just sit here for a few minutes, okay? No need to move."

Except I can't solve this case from this bench. Two women have been taken by the same crazy guy. If he struck again with Carmen, it could mean Maggie is already dead. And I have no idea who he is, where he's taken these women, or how he's choosing his victims. My head spins, and I pass out.

I wake up in my bed with Jezebel licking my face.

"Jez, no," Mitchell says, trying to shoo her away from the bed.

"It's okay," I tell him, trying to sit up. I move slowly in case the effects of my vision haven't worn off. I feel okay, though. "How long was I out?"

"Three hours. I filled your dad in. He's trying to find a connection between Maggie and Carmen so we can hopefully figure out if they both know the kidnapper from somewhere." The teakettle whistles, and Mitchell puts a finger in the air. "Be right back."

With him gone, I pat the bed next to me, letting Jezebel know it's okay for her to come up. She snuggles up next to me, putting her head on my chest and looking into my eyes. I'm not sure how I ever got along without her. She's the perfect companion.

Mitchell returns with a mug of tea for me. "Green tea with orange, passion fruit, and jasmine. No cream or sugar."

"Keep it up and Marcia will hire you to work in her store." I take the mug and breathe in the scent of the tea.

Mitchell sits down on the bed, closer than I'm comfortable with, but he reaches over and scratches Jezebel's head, so I'm assuming his intent is to pet her. I must be eyeing him, though, because he stands up and says, "Sorry. I didn't mean to crowd you. I've just gotten attached to this one." He motions to Jez.

"It's hard not to love her." I lean forward and kiss the top of her nose, and she thanks me by licking my nose in return.

"How are you feeling?" He shoves his hands into his pockets.

"Better. Did you wind up carrying me back to your car?" I ask, completely embarrassed by the idea and thankful I slept through the actual act.

"After you left me to take care of getting Peg and Shirley home, you deserved the embarrassment of me carrying you back to the car. Peg pinched my ass when I was leaving. It was humiliating."

I laugh. "Serves you right. You usually charm the women we come into contact with on these cases. Why should Peg and Shirley be any different?"

"First, they aren't part of the case. Second, they're old enough to be my grandmothers. Talk about forbidden fruit," he jokes.

"Wait a second. Maggie is married, so I can see how the kidnapper views her as forbidden. But what about Carmen? She lives alone."

"Maybe she's involved with someone."

I shake my head and put my tea down on the nightstand. "Colleen said Carmen would have told her if she was dating someone new. That means she doesn't have a boyfriend."

"You're right. So why is Carmen off-limits to this guy?"

We stare at each other for a moment, as if one of us will magically figure out the answer.

"Maybe she's secretly studying to be a nun," Mitchell says.

"Be serious. We don't know how much time we have before the kidnapper does something to her. If he hasn't already."

"Maybe we should call your dad. He can come here and help us brainstorm."

I throw the covers off me. "I'm not staying in bed all day just because I had a vision that knocked me out. I've been through this before."

"Yeah, but you were out cold, Piper. He must have used a ton of chloroform on Carmen if the vision affected you this much."

I start pacing the floor around the bed. "He'd only need to do that if he was taking her somewhere far away."

"So not in Weltunkin. That could mean he doesn't live here."

"It could, but then how does he know Maggie and Carmen? They weren't random targets. He knew Carmen's routine."

"We don't know that. He could have been hiding in that bush waiting to attack whomever sat on that bench."

I stop pacing and face him. "No. He knew her, watched her. He put that pomegranate in her car. And he knew Maggie's phone number. The attacks weren't random at all."

He doesn't question me. "Are you sure you're okay to go to the office?"

"Yes, but that's not where I want to go. I need to go back to Carmen's place. I have to figure out how she and Maggie are connected."

Since neither Maggie nor Carmen saw their attacker, I have nothing to go on there, which means I have to find out how the two women are connected in order to find any male acquaintances they both might share.

"I'll drive," Mitchell says. "I walked Jez a few minutes before she woke you up. I actually think she was trying to wake you to let you know she was a good girl for me."

I bend down, and Jez rushes over to me and sits. "Is that true? Were you good for Mitchell?"

She gives one sharp bark. I scratch her head. "Mommy will be back later, okay?" I stand up and take a deep breath. My dizziness has subsided, and the three-hour nap cured my tiredness, so I'm good to go. "Let's do this."

On the way, Mitchell calls Dad to fill him in on our plan.

"So far, I haven't found a link between the two women. They aren't friends on any social media outlets. Carmen doesn't even have a Saves-A-Lot club card, so it doesn't appear she shops there either. They never attended the same school. Carmen's lived in Weltunkin all her life, but Maggie moved here when she married Glen, whom she apparently met in college. She's originally from New Jersey, though. That's all I've got," Dad says with a sigh.

Neither one of them needs to tell me this is where I come in. Colleen is meeting us at Carmen's place to let us in. Then I need to read a bunch of things while focusing on Maggie, not Carmen, in hopes that there's a connection there. No pressure or anything. And since I never know how people will react to my abilities, I get to deal with having Colleen watch me have visions and hope she doesn't kick me out the way Glen Burns did.

I zone out, not even realizing Dad's voice is no longer coming through the Bluetooth in Mitchell's car.

"Hey." Mitchell eyes me briefly before turning his attention back to the road. "What's going on in that head of yours?"

"I was just thinking it might be easier to wear a name tag that says, 'Hi, my name is Piper, and I'm the psychic freak you may have heard about.' It could save me some time on these cases."

"You're not a freak. Most of the people who have been opposed to what you do reacted that way because they had something to hide. We can pretty much gauge who's guilty by their reaction to your abilities."

"Piper Ashwell, criminal detector."

"Hey, I wish I could do that. Think of how handy that would be for me."

More like he wishes he had my ability because he's dying to understand his mother. I'm convinced he doesn't have any psychic abilities, though.

He pulls into Carmen's driveway. Colleen is sitting on the front porch, waiting for us. Mitchell eyes me as we walk around the front of the Explorer to meet her. "Everything okay?" he asks Colleen.

"Yeah, it's just that going in there when I know she could be..." She shakes her head. "It's too difficult." She doesn't even attempt to get up when we reach her. "Would you mind if I stayed out here while you two do your thing inside?"

The news couldn't be better for me. "No problem at all. We understand," I say, placing my left hand on her shoulder, hoping it comes across as comforting since I don't have much experience with the notion.

"Is it open?" Mitchell asks.

Colleen nods. "Go right on in."

Mitchell opens the front door but steps aside to let me

enter first. Instead of going to the left into the living room like last time, I head for the stairs. I want to see Carmen's bedroom where she'll have more personal items.

"Any idea what we're looking for in particular?" Mitchell follows me up the stairs, cringing at the paisley wallpaper. "Man, this place needs some updating. Even I know this hasn't been fashionable in about fifty years."

"I'm surprised you know that considering you think the shirt you're wearing goes with that tie."

He stops at the top of the stairs and checks out his outfit. "What's wrong with this?"

"For one, you're mixing patterns, which begs the question, why are you even wearing a tie. They don't suit you. And two, you're wearing all black and brown, which is a color combination I've always hated."

"For your information, I lost a bet and that's why I'm wearing the tie."

"A bet with whom?" We've been working this case nonstop. When did he have time to even make a bet, let alone lose one?

He looks down at the green shag carpeting in the hallway. "Your father."

"Oh my God!" I should have recognized the tie sooner. "I bought that hideous thing when I was seven years old." It was a Father's Day gift. I was so proud because I earned my own money by helping my elderly neighbor with odd jobs like folding her laundry and dusting. That tie was on the clearance rack, and I thought it was the perfect gift since my dad always wore ties to work.

Mitchell picks up the bottom of the tie. "So it's your fault I look this awful today."

"No, it's yours. What exactly did you bet with my father?"

DRASTIC CRIMES CALL FOR DRASTIC INSIGHTS

"It's not important." He tries to walk around me, but I stick out my arms to block his path.

"Uh-uh. If he's making you wear that tie, then the bet must have had something to do with me. And if that's the case, I have a right to know."

"It's really no big deal. I actually forgot all about the bet because we made it so long ago."

I cross my arms. "So long ago? You've only been working with him and me on three cases. How long could it possibly have been?"

"You're not going to let this go, are you?"

"Nope. So start talking."

He huffs. "Fine. When I first became his partner, he was worried you were going to hate me."

"He wasn't wrong there, but go on." I wave my hand in the air to motion he should continue.

"Funny. Anyway, I told him there wasn't a woman alive that I couldn't charm."

Loud and uncontrolled laughter blurts out of me. I cover my mouth because if Colleen changed her mind and came inside, she'd think I was really insensitive for laughing while her friend is missing.

"I'm glad you're enjoying this, but truth be told, your dad was afraid he was losing the bet when he found out about our 'sleepovers.'"

"Don't call them that. It just makes you sound even more delusional." I remove my phone from my purse and snap a picture of him in the tie.

"Really, Piper? If you wanted my picture so badly, you could have just asked. You don't need to pretend it's for blackmail." He smirks. "Besides, I'm totally pulling off this look."

"Like I said, *delusional*." I pocket my phone and head

toward the first closed door on the right of the hallway. I turn the knob and open the door. It's a bedroom, but not the one I'm looking for. It's Carmen's childhood bedroom. At least I hope she doesn't still sleep in here with the pink flowered wallpaper and princess canopy bed.

"Yikes." Mitchell steps into the room behind me. "It's like this entire house is frozen in time."

"It's creepy, right?" I back out of the room. Nothing in here will help me because it's all too old. I turn for the door on the opposite side of the hallway, but it's a bathroom. "I guess that leaves this door as the master bedroom," I say, walking to the door at the end of the hallway.

"Good sleuthing," Mitchell mocks as I open the door.

This room isn't quite as outdated as the others considering there are actually items in it that don't predate this century. I walk past the dresser since there's no jewelry box or anything on top of it except a paperback that doesn't look like its spine has ever been cracked open. There's no clothing or anything on the floor, so I move toward the closet on the right wall.

I reach for the double doors and gently tug them. That's when I come face-to-face with a tall man in a leather jacket, a baseball cap, and black leather gloves.

CHAPTER NINE

"Freeze!" Mitchell has his gun trained on the man.

My hand is on my heart, which is pounding so hard I fear it might crack a rib. I stare at the man's face. Or lack of a face. "It's a mannequin." I pull the cap off the head to reveal the painted expression on the fair-skinned mannequin.

Mitchell puts his gun away. "Why would she keep a mannequin in her closet?"

I place the cap back on its head and reach for the leather glove on the mannequin's left hand. "No idea."

"Are those the same gloves you saw in your vision?" Mitchell asks.

At first, I thought so, and that's why my heart was beating so quickly. But now I see these gloves are different. They're more tapered. "No. Not a match."

"Do you think you could read them anyway, like you read that apple I bought?"

I try not to get upset that he still doesn't quite understand my abilities. "No. I can only try to replicate a vision

I've already seen that way. I can't call up anything new. It won't work."

"It was just a thought." He picks up the mannequin and places it to the right of the closet so we can look around inside.

Carmen has a huge collection of clothing ranging from ultra fancy to lounge clothes. "Well, it seems she inherited her fashion sense from one of her other relatives and not her parents. But I wonder why she never fixed up the house then?"

"Probably can't afford to. You know what it's like living in this town."

I do. I haven't so much as repainted my place. It's not a necessary expense. Plus I'm not home much, or I wasn't before I inherited Jezebel. I push some clothing aside to reveal a shelf in the back of the closet. A round leather bag sits in the center of the shelf. "Carmen's a bowler," I say, pulling out the bag.

"Think she and Maggie are on the same bowling team?" Mitchell asks, following me to the bed where I place the bag so I can unzip it.

"Could be." I peer inside at the deep purple ball. "Here goes nothing." I stick my fingers into the holes.

"You got lucky," a guy with a goatee and thinning brown hair says, returning his ball to its bag.

"You call whooping your ass lucky?" Carmen whistles. "Boy, Frank, it must be nice inside your head where the world always operates in a way that makes you look better. Out here in the real world, I made you look like the chump you are." She extends her hand to him, palm up. "Now pay up. Two hundred dollars."

"Come on. Double or nothing."

"Too rich for my blood." She wiggles her fingers. "Pay up."

Frank slaps two hundred-dollar bills on Carmen's palm. "One day, your luck is going to run out, and I'm going to be there to see it happen."

I open my eyes to see Mitchell staring at me.

"Sorry, I know you hate people watching you when you're doing that, but I've seen you collapse too many times to not look for signs of you passing out."

I rezip the bowling bag. "It's fine. I didn't sense Maggie at all. Although all I saw was some guy named Frank. Carmen beat him in a game, and she won two hundred dollars from him. He wasn't happy to have to pay her either."

"How unhappy are we talking? Enough to abduct her?"

"I can't be sure. I didn't get enough of a read on him."

"Then I guess we should check him out. Was Carmen in a bowling league or something?"

"No. I think it was just a one-on-one match."

"Could you tell if it was the Weltunkin bowling alley?"

"Considering the guy was carrying around crisp one hundred dollar bills, I'd say it probably was."

"Want to go there and ask around about him? I'm sure one of the workers would at least know the guy by sight if not by name. I'm assuming you can describe him."

Sometimes I experience visions from a person's perspective, which means I can't see what they look like. But that wasn't the case this time. It was like I was watching a movie. "Yeah, I can. Let's look around here a little bit more first, though. I don't want to make poor Colleen keep coming back here to let us in."

"Yeah, she seems pretty upset." Mitchell returns the bowling bag to the back of the closet and starts rifling through the shoe rack next. "Doesn't look like she hid any jewelry or anything in her shoes. That's a common location for people to hide things."

"She doesn't appear to have any jewelry at all. That's odd." My eyes return to the mannequin. "Unless."

"Unless what?" Mitchell stops his search and stares at me.

I position myself in front of the mannequin, my fingers touching the mannequin's arm, and close my eyes. *Come on, Carmen. Where do you hide things you don't want others to find?* It takes a moment, but then Carmen's image comes to me.

She stands in front of her closet and smiles at the mannequin. "Good evening, George. Fine weather we're having today, don't you think?" She smiles to herself and reaches for George's head, lifting it straight off the body. She flips his head upside down and twists off the bottom cap to reveal a hidden storage area.

I open my eyes and grab the mannequin's face. "Sorry, George," I say before lifting the head right off.

"George?" Mitchell asks.

I twist off the cap from the base of the head. "That's what Carmen calls him."

"Man, this case is so screwed up." He leans over my shoulder to peer inside the hidden compartment with me.

My fingers are just slim enough to reach two inside and pull out a hundred dollar bill. And another. And another. And another.

"Whoa. Does she not believe in banks?" Mitchell asks, taking the money from me so I can keep pulling out the bills. Once I have about two thousand dollars freed from the head, I hear a tinkling sound. I tip the head over, letting the remaining contents spill into my open hand.

"Diamond earrings." I put the head back on the mannequin and examine the earrings.

"They have to be at least two karats each," Mitchell says. "Why would someone who doesn't wear jewelry have earrings like this?"

"Maybe they were her mother's or grandmother's," I suggest.

"Or maybe she won those, too. Do you think she hustles people in bowling?"

Something about his theory rings true to me. I take one diamond earring in my right hand.

"Why do you keep betting me, Frank? It's your own fault, really. You let your damn pride get in the way of what should be clear to you. I'm a better bowler than you are."

"Those are a present for my wife's birthday. You have to let me go double or nothing." Frank's face is bright red.

"I told you two hundred dollars was too much to go double or nothing on, yet you think I can do that for diamond earrings?" She swipes them from his hand. "You really have to be smarter than that, Frank."

"One of these days, Carmen, I will get my revenge on you."

As soon as the vision fades away, I turn to Mitchell. "We need to find this Frank guy. Now."

———

Twenty minutes later, Mitchell pulls into the parking lot of the bowling alley. Before we left, I returned the money and earrings to the mannequin head. While Colleen is voluntarily letting us into Carmen's place, she legally doesn't have the right to since she doesn't live there, so I don't want to do anything stupid like remove expensive items from the house. I have all I need to confront Frank with anyway.

Mitchell parks near the door, and we immediately head inside. Since it's Monday night, it's not too crowded. I motion toward the shoe rental, thinking everyone who comes in will go there, and that makes it the perfect place to ask questions about Frank.

There's a woman working the counter, so I nudge Mitchell. "You're up. Do your thing."

"Are you actually telling me to put on the Brennan charm to get information from that woman?"

Before he can get too excited, I reach for his tie and remove it. "You don't need anything else working against you." I shove the tie inside my purse, intent on having a talk with Dad about making bets that have to do with me. I'm thinking tomorrow at Ashwell family dinner night will be the perfect time to bring it up. I'm sure Mom will want to chime in on the subject.

While Mitchell approaches the woman, I hang back and take the opportunity to look around the place. The chairs aren't the typical plastic you find in bowling alleys. They're cushioned. And the carpeting looks like it was just vacuumed. As far as bowling alleys go, this one is really nice.

I see a guy with a spray bottle and rag cleaning the displays where people type in their names before playing. Since Mitchell is occupied, I walk over to the man.

"Excuse me."

He looks up but continues scrubbing the display. "Can I help you?"

"Yes. I was wondering if Frank is here tonight."

The guy stands up straight. "You know Frank?"

"Sort of. A friend of mine does. Carmen Ramon."

"I don't know last names, but I know a Carmen. She's quite the bowler. She's got a reputation around here."

"How so?" I ask, looking around him at the shoe rental where Mitchell is leaning on the counter and the woman is leaning right back at him like they're in the middle of an intimate conversation.

"No one can beat her. Frank sure tries like hell, but he's yet to actually do it. He came close once when Carmen had an allergic reaction to this new cleaner we were using. She was sneezing all through that game. She threw the one and only gutter ball I've ever seen her throw. Frank thought he had her that night, but he still lost. Big too. I'm not sure why he always bets so much."

The guy bowling in the next lane steps toward us. "He bets that much because she won't play him otherwise."

"You know Frank and Carmen?" I ask him. He looks like he's in his fifties. Still in great shape, which can't possibly be from bowling.

"Yeah. They're here every Friday night. And it's the same song and dance every time, too. Frank begs her to give him another chance to beat her. She turns him down repeatedly until he comes up with something to bet that she really wants. It's usually money, except for the time she played for those diamond earrings." He tsks. "She's a piece of work. I think she lets him get close to beating her every once in a while just to keep him coming back. A con artist, I'm telling you."

"Does Frank ever come in any other day during the week or only on Fridays?"

"On occasion, but like I said, he's usually looking for Carmen and that's the only night she's ever here."

"You don't happen to know Frank's last name, do you?"

The guy laughs. "I don't even know his real first name."

I narrow my eyes at him. "What do you mean? You've been calling him Frank this whole time."

"Because that's what it says on his bowling shirt. That's not his name, though."

Damn it. How am I supposed to find this guy, who is the most likely suspect for kidnapping Carmen, if I don't even know his first name?

CHAPTER TEN

After spending my night sketching Frank while recalling a vision, courtesy of the hundred-dollar bill in Mitchell's wallet, I get some much needed sleep. I know the Weltunkin PD will run the sketch through the system to see if we get a match.

But even after a solid eight hours of sleep, my mind is still restless. I have zero leads on Maggie Burns. My only hope is finding this "Frank" person and discovering he knows Maggie as well as Carmen. If not, I'm officially sunk. My senses are telling me the kidnapper wouldn't be taking multiple women at once if he's working on his own, and I'm certain he doesn't have a partner. So what is he doing with the women? If his end game is to kill them, then Maggie's already dead and Carmen will be soon if she isn't already.

My office door opens, and Mitchell and Dad walk in together, laughing. I open my bottom desk drawer and remove the hideous tie that's still in my purse. I slam it down on Dad's oversized desk. So much for waiting until dinner. "Most fathers keep the ugly gifts their children give them in a box in the back of their closets. They don't force their daughter's work partner to wear said ugly item in her presence."

"Pumpkin—"

I hold up my hand. "And, most fathers don't make bets about their daughter's..." I almost say love life, but that isn't right at all since I don't have one. Mitchell is eyeing me, waiting to see how I'll finish that sentence. "Choice of friends."

"Aw." Mitchell places both hands above his heart. "Did you just call me your friend?"

"Excuse the misuse of the word. I haven't had any coffee yet this morning."

"I'll go next door and get some," Mitchell says, walking out before I can protest. Or maybe he just doesn't want to witness any more of this conversation between Dad and me.

"Sorry, pumpkin. I thought it would be funny to bet Mitchell. I knew his little tricks would never work on you. Besides, the guys at the station always pull pranks on their new partners. It was par for the course."

"Fine, but did you have to bring me into it?"

Dad puts the tie in his desk drawer and shrugs. "He was always talking about you. It just popped into my head."

"Well, don't let it happen again," I say, sounding more like the parent than the child in this relationship.

Dad laughs. "I actually thought I was going to lose the bet a few times."

"That's—"

"Say what you will, Piper, but working with Mitchell has been good for you. When you don't realize you're doing it, you actually let him in. I don't think calling him your friend a few minutes ago was a slipup at all."

"Marcia's my friend. Jezebel is my friend. That's enough for me."

"Jezebel is a dog. Oh, and before I forget, your mom said Jez is invited to dinner tonight. She thinks it will be good for Max to play with another dog while we eat. He's been bored lately."

"How can you tell when a dog is bored?" I ask.

Dad shrugs and opens his laptop. "Beats me, but your mother is certain he is. She even bought him special bones and everything. She put a Post-it note on the package that says, 'For when he's bored,' as if I have a clue when that is." He shakes his head. "Anyway, I'm checking Carmen's social media to see if anyone named Frank follows her there."

"I doubt it. They aren't exactly friends. In fact, I'm pretty sure Frank hates her." I drum my fingers on the top of my desk. "I just don't know if he hates her enough to harm her."

Dad cocks his head at me. "What's your gut telling you?"

"That I need to find Frank as soon as possible." That's all my senses are conveying. Not that he actually did anything, though. Maybe he hired someone to do his dirty work for him.

Mitchell returns with coffee and muffins from Marcia's Nook, and he's smiling so wide it's making me nauseated.

"What's got you in such a good mood?" I ask, reaching for my large coffee from the carrier. I always know which one is mine because Marcia writes my name on it, knowing I'm the only one of us who drinks toasted almond.

"Marcia. She knows you too well."

Great. Marcia and Mitchell are talking about me behind my back? I don't like this at all. "Do I dare ask?"

Mitchell sits down and opens the clear plastic container of four muffins. "First, two of these bad boys are mine, so hands off."

They're coffee crumble muffins, one of my favorites. "We'll see about that. Now start talking."

Mitchell grabs a muffin, takes a huge bite of it, spilling crumbs on his lap, and moans. "That's good," he says with his mouth full.

"You're a pig."

He swallows and gives his best pig grunt. "So, Marcia asked what I did to piss you off enough that I felt the need to not only flee your office but go get you coffee and food."

She is good, and at least they weren't really talking about me then. More like discussing Mitchell's annoying qualities. "What can I say? She's smart."

"No followers named Frank," Dad says, pushing his laptop aside to reach for his muffin and coffee.

I take a few sips of my coffee before digging into a muffin. "Did you check Maggie's social media accounts, too? Maybe he follows her."

"Good thinking," Dad says, pulling his laptop back to him.

I easily could have checked myself, but these days Dad prefers office work to fieldwork, so any computer-related research has become his territory.

Mitchell and I race to finish our muffins and see who gets to claim the fourth one still sitting in the container. We finish at the same time and both reach for it. Dad huffs, smacks both our hands, and then pulls a plastic knife out of a box in his top desk drawer. "You two are like children fighting over a toy."

"Not big on toys. Food on the other hand..." Mitchell eyes the muffin as Dad cuts it in half.

"Don't even tell me I cut one side bigger," Dad says, giving us each an admonishing glare. Mitchell and I remain silent as Dad dishes the muffin halves, probably anticipating

DRASTIC CRIMES CALL FOR DRASTIC INSIGHTS

we'd fight over who got which half. "There. Now, in the words of my kindergarten teacher, 'you get what you get, and you don't get upset.'"

Something about Dad's words triggers a vision. I close my eyes and allow it to fill my mind.

"Ricky threw a fit in class today when Jacob got the instrument he wanted during music." The woman places her purse on the kitchen table.

"Ricky always throws fits," Frank says, opening the refrigerator and grabbing a bottle of Blue Moon from the door.

"I know, so I looked him straight in the eye and said, 'You get what you get, and you don't get upset.' Oddly enough, it worked."

"And that's why you're the best kindergarten teacher in Weltunkin."

I open my eyes and blurt out, "Frank's wife is a kindergarten teacher here in Weltunkin."

"There are three schools in the area with kindergarten classes," Dad says.

"Pull them up. I know what she looks like, so as long as they have staff photos, I'll find her. Then we can get her name and address."

"And go interrogate Frank," Mitchell finishes for me.

The first two schools Dad pulls up don't have any teachers who look like Frank's wife, so he pulls up the last one and turns the laptop screen toward me. I recognize her immediately. Her blonde curly hair and blue eyes stare back at me.

"Sara Ackerman. That's her." I point to the screen.

Dad copies the image and then gets started tracking her down online while Mitchell and I eat.

"How did you do that?" Mitchell asks. "You didn't even have anything to read to provoke that vision."

"It was what Dad said. Sara was telling Frank about a student in class who got upset with the instrument he was given during music class. She told him, 'You get what you get, and you don't get upset.'"

"So basically, the two of you acting like children spurred the vision," Dad says, his fingers clicking away on the laptop keyboard.

"Happy to help," Mitchell says with a smile.

"It wasn't a compliment or pat on the back." I roll my eyes and wheel my chair closer to Dad's so I can read the screen as he works. He has her Facebook profile pulled up, and there under her information, it shows her marital status. "Married to Christopher Ackerman."

Dad clicks on Christopher's name, but the profile it brings up doesn't even have a photo. "He clearly never uses this."

"It's possible Sara set it up for him without consulting him first," I say. "Doesn't matter, though. Now we can find out where they live because we have both of their names."

"I'm on it." Dad starts typing away again.

I finish my muffin half and toss the napkin I was using as a plate into the trash can. "What are the odds Christopher will be home on a Tuesday morning?"

"Probably not good," Mitchell says. "Want to spend some time looking into Maggie some more and wait until later to pay the Ackermans a visit?"

I open my laptop and search for connections between Maggie Burns and Sara Ackerman. I keep the screen tilted so Mitchell can see what I'm doing.

"Good thinking," he says.

"One of us has to be the brains of this operation." I

search all the social media sites and do a Google search, but I come up with exactly nothing. Another dead end.

Dad scribbles something on a Post-it note. "Here's the address. Mitchell's right, though. You're better off looking into Maggie some more and waiting until dinnertime to go see Christopher Ackerman."

Mitchell leans back in his seat. "I guess that means there won't be an Ashwell family dinner tonight."

"Oh, there will be, but you won't be invited," I say.

"Actually, I'll have your mother postpone, and you both can come when you're finished talking to Christopher."

Mitchell's face lights up. "I like that plan. See, Piper, the position of 'brains of the operation' has already been filled by your dad. You can be our token eye roller who likes to make sarcastic comments."

"Awesome. Although, if you'd stop being such an ass, I wouldn't do either of those things half as much."

Dad sighs and laces his hands behind his head. "You two are going to make me go bald."

"You have plenty of hair on your head, Dad." I pat the side of his head.

"Now, but you two make me want to rip it all out. Why don't you go talk to Glen Burns some more? See what you can find out about Maggie that might help you figure out if Christopher Ackerman is the one who assaulted her." He shoos us with both hands.

I slip my jacket on and stand up. "You heard the man. Let's go." I walk past Mitchell with my car keys in hand, but he jumps up and says, "I'm driving."

I don't bother to argue. I actually hate driving, mostly because if I have a vision behind the wheel, I'd probably get myself and possibly others killed. "Fine. You can chauffer me around town."

He reaches around me to open the office door.

"Good luck!" Dad calls after us.

Mitchell calls the police station on the way to Maggie's house to tell them we've located Christopher Ackerman. He also finds out Glen was released because Tanner decided to drop the assault charges. That seems odd to me.

"Maybe we should talk to Tanner again, too. Find out why he's not pressing charges anymore."

"Do you think Glen threatened him?" Mitchell asks. "Or is there a possibility Glen hired Tanner to abduct his wife?"

"No. Despite the affair, Glen loves Maggie. I don't understand how that's possible, but it's what I'm sensing. He's seriously messed up." I look out the passenger window of the Explorer, watching the scenery zip by.

"Okay, then what could it be?" I know he's hoping I'll just spit out the answer, but nothing comes to me.

I shrug even though I'm not facing him and can't be sure he even sees it.

When we pull up to Glen and Maggie's house, there are no cars in the driveway. I don't sense Glen either. "He's not here," I say.

"Do you want to track him down at work or go see Tanner?"

"Tanner. He should be working at Saves-A-Lot. We can talk to him, and if necessary, I'll try to read Maggie's locker again."

Mitchell barely seems like he's paying attention to me, and I follow his gaze to the front porch. There's a basket on it. I don't know why, but I feel drawn to it. I open the car door and step out. Mitchell does the same, but he doesn't say a word. He knows I'm onto something and doesn't want to distract me.

I walk up the front porch steps and bend down. The basket has a bouquet of flowers and a fresh fruit salad. Between the two is a card. I look up at Mitchell, knowing it's not legal to read someone else's mail, but this isn't necessarily mail. The person who sent it could have dropped it off in person, making it a gift, not a delivery per se.

"I'm just going to turn around and admire this quiet neighborhood some." Mitchell puts his back to me.

I reach for the card and slip it out of the white envelope.

Maggie,

Thank you so much for all of your help with the children's Sunday school pageant. I don't know how we would have done it without you. You're a Godsend.

Emily

I return the card to the envelope and stand up. "It's from someone at Maggie's church," I say. "Apparently, they don't know she's missing."

"It's a big town, though you'd think if they were close, they'd notice Maggie didn't show up on Sunday."

That's true, especially since the card mentioned Sunday school. I didn't get any bad vibes from the note, though. If I had, I would have read the energy off it instead of just reading what Emily wrote in the card itself.

Mitchell's phone rings the moment we get back inside the Explorer. He answers via the Bluetooth.

"You two aren't going to believe this," Dad says.

"What?" I ask, clicking my seat belt.

"Christopher Ackerman plays poker every Saturday night with Tanner Montgomery."

"Montgomery could have told Ackerman about Maggie," Mitchell says.

"There's our connection between Ackerman and both missing women."

CHAPTER ELEVEN

I feel like we have our first real lead. We found a common ground between the two victims. It's small, but it could be exactly what we need to break this case.

"Dad, I need to know where Ackerman works."

"I figured as much. He's a lawyer at the Walsh law firm on Main Street."

A lawyer? You've got to be kidding me.

"That's the perfect cover," Mitchell says, already en route to Main Street. "No one suspects the lawyer of being the one to break the law, but there he is gambling at his poker game and at the bowling alley."

"And it explains why he uses a fake name at the bowling alley," I add. "But how does he know no one will recognize him from the law firm?"

"Maybe he's taking a gamble no one will," Mitchell says, earning a look of disgust from me. His cheesy jokes have got to stop. "What? It makes sense."

"We're on our way there now. Thanks, Dad. We'll keep you posted."

Mitchell disconnects the call. "Is your Spidey sense tingling at this connection?"

"I don't know if it's that or just elation at finally having a worthwhile lead to follow."

"We'll know soon enough. You do plan to read him upon introduction, right?"

"Well, fortune telling is illegal in the state of Pennsylvania, but that's not really what I do."

"You're worried he'll sue you?"

"He's a lawyer and possibly an abductor and/or killer. I'm not putting anything past him."

"Then maybe we keep that part of your job description a secret. You're a private investigator. You have a degree. He doesn't need to know how you obtain your information."

Great. Yet another person I have to hide my abilities from. I hate having to pretend I'm something I'm not, in this case a normal, average private investigator.

The Walsh law firm is located in a high-rise on the corner of Main Street. Mitchell finds a parking spot, and we take the elevator to the law office on the fifth floor. When the elevator opens, we're greeted by a young woman seated at a large receptionist desk. She looks like she's fresh out of college.

"Can I help you?" she asks us, her gaze going right to Mitchell.

He leans against the desk and smiles at her. "I certainly hope so. We're here to speak with Christopher Ackerman."

"Do you have an appointment?" the woman asks in a sweet voice.

"Actually no." Mitchell leans closer and lowers his voice, not in volume but in pitch. I huff behind him, but he doesn't seem to notice. "You see, I'm Detective Mitchell Brennan." He pulls his badge out from under his jacket.

"My partner and I need to speak with Mr. Ackerman about a case we're investigating."

"I see. One moment please." She stands up and walks to a door about a hundred feet behind her desk. She looks back over her shoulder and smiles at Mitchell before knocking.

Once she's inside the office, I smack Mitchell's arm. "What is wrong with you? Can't you do anything without flirting?"

"Hey, I got the job done, didn't I?"

"That's yet to be seen. Ackerman is behind that door, and we're still standing out here."

Mitchell opens his mouth to reply, but the blonde receptionist comes back out to us. She addresses Mitchell as if I'm not even here. "I'm so sorry, Detective, but I'm afraid Mr. Ackerman will be tied up all afternoon. He said you're welcome to schedule something for tomorrow."

I nudge Mitchell aside. "Let me," I tell him before addressing Blondie. "Hi. Could you please give Mr. Ackerman a quick message for me? I'm certain he's going to want to speak with us after you do."

"I highly doubt that, and if I disturb him again, I could lose my job."

Mitchell pushes me aside this time and leans forward on the desk. "We definitely wouldn't want to get you in any trouble with your boss, but it would mean a lot to me if you could just relay a brief message to him."

She tucks a strand of hair behind her ear and bites her lower lip. "I guess I can deliver a message if it's a quick one."

Good Lord, if I have to endure this for one more second... "Please tell him we need to talk to him about Frank's gambling problem," I say loudly enough to break the trance Mitchell's put on the receptionist. If that doesn't get Ackerman's attention, nothing will.

Mitchell places his hand on top of Blondie's. "We'd really appreciate it."

She holds up one finger and says, "One moment." Her walk back to the office is clearly meant for Mitchell's benefit.

"I've never seen someone sway their hips that much without falling over."

"Not everyone is as uncoordinated as you, Piper," Mitchell says, leaning an elbow on top of the desk. "Nice work mentioning Frank's gambling problem, by the way."

"Well, one of us had to stay focused on our actual job."

The office door opens, and Blondie says, "Mr. Ackerman will see you now." She remains in the doorway as we walk past her into the office. Her eyes take in Mitchell's full form as he brushes past her.

Christopher Ackerman stands up, adjusts his plain black tie, and motions for us to take the empty seats across from his mahogany desk. He doesn't speak until Blondie closes the door. "Detectives, what can I do for you? And let me apologize for needing to make this brief. I do have a packed schedule today."

"We don't anticipate needing much of your time," I say, sitting down. "I'm Piper Ashwell, and this is Detective Brennan. We're here because Carmen Ramon is missing."

"Who?" Ackerman furrows his brow as if he's never heard the name before, but the way he's clicking the pen in his right hand tells me differently.

"The woman you like to bowl with on Friday nights. And when I say 'like' I actually mean you hope to finally beat so you can make back some of the money and the diamond earrings for your wife that you gambled away."

Ackerman drops the pen onto his desk and leans

forward, keeping his voice low. "What is this? Are you trying to blackmail me?"

"You think a police detective would stoop so low as to blackmail you?" Then again, he's a lawyer with gambling problems.

"What do you want then?"

"Do you know where Carmen is?" Mitchell asks.

"I haven't seen her since Friday night at the bowling alley." Ackerman is still speaking in a hushed tone, making me wonder how thin the office walls are and whether or not his colleagues are occupying their offices at the moment as well.

"And what about Tanner Montgomery?" Mitchell asks.

"What about him?"

"You play poker with him every Saturday," I say much louder than necessary.

Ackerman leans forward and presses a finger to his lips. "Please keep your voice down."

"I'd be happy to once I know we have your full cooperation." I lace my hands in my lap.

"Fine. You've got it, okay? Tanner is just some punk kid who joined our weekly game. I don't ever talk to him outside of that environment."

"Does he talk about work while you play?" Mitchell asks.

"Some, I guess. I don't pay much attention to the guy. He's not very good, and it usually only takes a few hands to wipe him out of cash each week."

"Is that the money you wind up losing to Carmen on Friday nights?" I ask.

Ackerman's face turns red. "Usually," he says through gritted teeth.

"I get the sense you don't care much for Carmen," Mitchell says.

"You think I did something to her?" Ackerman scoffs. "I'll tell you this. If she's missing, it's probably because she scammed someone out of a lot of money and they retaliated."

"That was my thought, too," I say. "But the only person we know of that she took money from is you." With my fingers still laced, I dip my hands forward and point both thumbs at him.

"I'm telling you I didn't do anything to that woman."

"The problem is you might be the last person to have seen her," Mitchell says. "She disappeared sometime between Friday night and Monday morning."

I resist the urge to give Mitchell a questioning look since we know Carmen was assaulted on one of her morning runs.

"Look. If she was hustling me, she was most likely doing the same to someone else. Go find that person."

"Except she wasn't hustling you," I say. "You sought her out because you were determined to beat her."

"Maybe. So what? I have a little thing called pride. That's not a crime. I'd know."

"No, but it is one of the seven deadly sins."

Mitchell eyes me, and even I'm not sure why I said that.

"Do you know Maggie Burns?" I ask.

Ackerman's body tenses, giving himself away.

"I know you do, so you might as well tell us the truth."

"She hired one of my colleagues to draw up divorce papers to serve her husband. She recently discovered he's having an affair."

So she does know about Glen's extracurricular activities.

"Except the irony of the situation is that she wound up sleeping with my colleague."

"She's having an affair, too?" Mitchell asks, his voice laced with shock.

"Not just one. He found out she's sleeping with multiple men. I guess the news about her husband sent her on a payback mission. She doesn't want to just leave him. She wants to outdo him in the infidelity department."

God, what is wrong with people?

Lust.

I shake my head, clearing it of the word that popped into my mind as if in answer to my internal question. "Mr. Ackerman, you're sure you haven't seen either woman in the past few days?"

"I've never even met Maggie. I saw her come here once, but that was it. And like I said, the last I saw Carmen was Friday night."

My senses are telling me he's speaking the truth, so I stand up. "Thank you for your time. We won't hold you up any longer."

Mitchell gets up, but I can tell he's not happy I just ended the interrogation.

"Detectives," Ackerman calls after us. "You'll leave my name out of this investigation, right? Both my names?"

There's no need to bring him into this. He might not be a standup lawyer, but he's not responsible for either woman's disappearance.

"You can consider your involvement in this matter closed," I say, opening the door and seeing myself out.

The receptionist hands Mitchell a business card as we walk past, and I don't need to ask to know the scribble on the back is her phone number. I press the button for the elevator.

We don't even make it downstairs before Mitchell's phone rings. "Brennan," he answers. "You're kidding. No, I don't. Send me the details." He hangs up.

"What is it?" I ask, stepping out of the elevator.

"We've got another missing woman."

CHAPTER TWELVE

Despite Mom's rule of not discussing work at the dinner table, Mitchell, Dad, and I can't seem to talk about anything else. While Mitchell and I fill Dad in on what we discovered at the law office, she glares at each of us, but when that doesn't work, she eats in silence, only talking to Max and Jezebel, who are both sitting beside her, begging for food.

"Twenty-two-year-old Sky Lucas was walking her dogs in the park." Mitchell uses the side of his fork to cut his lasagna. "Well, not *her* dogs. She's a dog walker, so the dogs belonged to other people."

"We get it. Go on." I wave my fork in the air, not concerned by tiny details that don't mean anything to the case.

"The dogs were found wandering the park, their leashes just dragging on the ground behind them. No sign of Sky anywhere. Her boyfriend reported her missing when she didn't come home or answer her phone four hours after leaving with the dogs."

"Does she live with her boyfriend?" Dad asks.

Mitchell nods as he swallows a bite of lasagna.

"How did no one at the park see anything?" I ask. "I mean, I guess I can see how Carmen was taken, which was at the same park but early in the morning. Plus, we know the attacker was waiting in the bushes, concealed from view. But Sky was out during the day. There had to be young kids and stay-at-home moms and dads around."

"It might mean Sky knew her attacker," Mitchell offers before taking a sip of lemonade.

"Okay, but then how did he get her to abandon the dogs? That part still wouldn't make sense."

"They could have been tied up somewhere and got free when Sky didn't return for them," Dad says.

"The park has that fenced in area for dogs, though. Wouldn't she put them in there?" I ask, and immediately dismiss my own idea. "She would have removed their leashes first, so the fact that the dogs still had their leashes when they were found means she didn't do that."

"So we're back to her tying them up somewhere," Dad says.

"Thomas, Piper clearly isn't sensing that's what happened," Mom says, setting her empty glass of iced tea on the table with nothing left but the squished lemon wedge. "Try the game."

I take a deep breath because we really don't have any other options. Of course, not having ever held anything that belonged to Sky is going to make this game nearly impossible.

"Hang on," Mitchell says, removing the napkin from his lap and placing it on the table beside his plate. He leaves the room and returns a few minutes later with Jezebel's leash. "I know it's not actually related to the case, but I thought it couldn't hurt to try holding this while your dad questions you."

"It's a good idea. Thanks," I say, taking the leash. Jezebel, thinking we're going for a walk, comes to my side and sits down, her tail wagging back and forth on the floor. "Not now, sweet girl. Mommy needs to borrow your leash for something first. Lie down like a good girl, and I'll walk you when I'm finished."

She slides her front paws forward until she's lying down. Then she places her head on my right foot.

Dad puts down his fork and meets my gaze. I have to have a clear mind before he can start asking me random questions I already know the answers to. Then he'll throw in questions specific to the case in hopes that my mind will call forth an answer to those as well.

I nod to let him know I'm ready.

"Are you enjoying your mother's lasagna?" he starts.

"Yes."

"Are you hoping she does the dishes so you don't have to?"

"Yes."

"Will Jezebel be sleeping in bed with you tonight?"

"Yes."

"Did Sky tie the dogs up somewhere at the park?"

"Yes."

"Where did she tie them?"

"To the water fountain by the restrooms."

"How did they get free?"

"A kid untied them when he got a drink of water."

"Do you know who attacked Sky?"

"No."

"Can you picture her in the restroom?"

"No."

I open my eyes. "That's all I've got. Sorry, Dad."

"Don't apologize, pumpkin. You did great."

More like if this were a child's competition, I'd get a participation award rather than a ribbon for first, second, or third place.

"Tying up the dogs so she could use the restroom definitely makes sense," Mitchell says, thinking aloud.

Jezebel stands up and nudges the leash in my hand.

"I did promise, didn't I?" I stand up, my gaze going to Mom. "Do you mind if I go take Jez for a walk? I'll help you clean up when I get back."

Mom waves her hand in the air. "Go. And take Mitchell with you. Your father and I can handle loading the dishwasher."

"Thanks," I say, putting the leash on Jezebel.

Mitchell grabs both our jackets from the hall closet and hands mine to me. "Can you believe it will be winter soon?"

"Don't remind me. I hate the cold." I put the jacket on and open the front door. It's been a very mild fall, and I'm hoping the weather continues to cooperate throughout the winter, but with Thanksgiving fast approaching, I'm not sure how much longer this will last.

Jez leads the way down the street. This dog loves her walks, which reminds me I need to have Dad work his magic on Mr. Hall so I don't have to hide Jezebel anymore.

"Your abilities are expanding," Mitchell says.

"They are. I still can't see the future, though. Not for anything significant, at least."

"That's okay. I'm kind of convinced seeing the future doesn't mean you can prevent it from happening." He shoves his hands into the pockets of his coat and looks down at the sidewalk.

"You might be right, and in that case, it must make that particular gift really tough to have."

Mitchell's head lowers. "I think she saw it as a punishment."

That's an awful way to think of it. As if Jez can sense Mitchell is upset, she falls into step with him and nudges his hand with her head. Who knows? Maybe dog's can have extrasensory abilities, too. Mitchell scratches the top of her head.

"Do you ever think of getting a dog of your own?" I ask him. "You're really great with Jez."

"Nah. I'm never home. Besides, you let me walk Jez, and since we're always together, it's almost like..." He clears his throat. "Not that I'm implying..." He looks up at the sky. "Hey, full moon. Look at that."

I laugh. "You rattle too easily. That doesn't bode well for your line of work."

"That's why I have you. Nothing rattles you."

"Yeah, right." He's seen me completely shaken up from visions I've had.

"Seriously. You and my mom are the strongest people I've ever met, and I think it's because of your abilities."

"Maybe, but you don't need psychic abilities to be strong. You've proven that." Now it's my turn to look away. I don't do the whole "share your feelings" thing well. "Any clue who took these women, Detective?"

"Uh-oh. Reverting to titles instead of first names. I thought I crossed that barrier with you back in October."

"Yeah, well, you jump to a lot of conclusions."

Jezebel stops to smell a tree, and Mitchell and I awkwardly stare anywhere but at each other.

"What's the plan for tomorrow?" Mitchell asks, and I'm relieved to be discussing the case again.

"Dad attempts to find a connection between Sky and the other two women while you and I check out that restroom at the park to see if something happened to Sky while she was in there."

Mitchell places his hand on his heart. "Piper, are you asking me on a date to a disgusting public restroom?" he says with mock sweetness.

"Nothing's too good for you."

―――

Equipped with coffee, Mitchell and I show up at the park at 7:00 a.m. I'm hoping to check out the bathroom before the daily crowd of walkers and moms with toddlers shows up. We head straight for the public restrooms located in the center of the park. I spot the water fountain where the dogs were tied up. It's metal, which means it's an easy object to read, but I don't want to have a vision of the dogs. I need to see Sky, which means I need to go inside the bathroom.

"Will you stand watch out here?" I ask Mitchell. I'd rather not have someone walk in on me while I'm in the middle of a vision.

"I think I should go inside with you. Who knows what you'll see?" His worried expression does nothing to ease my nerves.

"You can't come inside the women's restroom. I'll be fine."

He cocks his head at me.

"If I'm not out in five minutes, you can come in. That's my best offer."

He nods but doesn't look the least bit happy about the arrangement.

I push open the door and step into the restroom. It's brick with gray marble tile flooring. And it looks like the place was recently cleaned. Hopefully not too well since I need to get a read off of something Sky touched. Since I don't know which stall she used, and the prospect of reading a toilet is enough to make me want to vomit, I opt for the paper towel dispenser on the wall near the door.

"Here goes nothing," I say, clearing my mind and closing my eyes as I raise my right hand to the dispenser.

Sky stares at her reflection in the bathroom mirror as she washes her hands. "Stupid Tamara. How is it fair that she landed a cushy office job right after graduation and I'm stuck picking up dog crap? She always has everything handed to her. That should have been me."

She walks over to the paper towel dispenser. The stall door behind her opens as she dries her hands, and a moment later, something sharp is pressed against her back under the hem of her jacket.

"Don't move. Don't even speak. You're going to walk out of here with me like nothing is wrong, or I'll drive this knife right into your spine. Do you understand? Nod your head."

Sky nods, her entire body gripped with fear and one thought: This would never happen to Tamara.

CHAPTER THIRTEEN

When the vision ends, I rub my lower back and inspect it as if expecting to see a cut from the knife. I can't seem to get my brain to understand that what I experience in a vision isn't real. I take a few deep breaths to compose myself before opening the door and exiting the restroom. Mitchell is waiting directly outside, and I nearly bump right into him.

"Jeez." I glare at him as I walk over to the water fountain.

"Sorry. I was guarding the door, though. Some people started to arrive." He motions to the cars in the parking lot across the park. "How did it go?"

"She was jumped from behind. The guy came out of a stall while she was drying her hands. He held a knife to her back."

"Did you see who attacked her?"

"No. I witnessed the vision from Sky's perspective, and like I said, she was attacked from behind."

"Did you get a sense that she knew the guy, though?"

"I couldn't tell. Sorry." I start walking toward Mitchell's Explorer.

"Would you stop apologizing? You're the only one keeping these cases moving forward."

"Am I though? Maggie's been missing for days. We have no new information about who took her. And now we can add two more women to the list. I'm not getting anywhere, and the missing persons just keep piling up." My chest is heaving. The pressure of this case is nearly crushing me. "I don't want to add three more names to the list of people I couldn't save."

Mitchell stops walking and grabs my arm. "I don't like losing people either. We're doing everything we can. Let's go back to the office and hope your dad found some connection between all three women. And if that connection turns out to be Christopher Ackerman, I'll find some reason to detain him. At least then if the kidnappings stop, we'll know we've got our guy."

Except I don't think Ackerman did this. I haven't gotten a sense of this person at all. Each assault was different, and that's totally screwing me up.

"No connection to Ackerman," Dad says the second we walk into the office. "The women don't seem to have any connection to each other either."

"Nothing matches up. I've never seen a serial abductor who didn't stick to any sort of pattern. Even the women he took couldn't be more different." Mitchell rubs the two-day scruff on his chin as he takes a seat opposite my desk.

"Not to mention the method of kidnapping," Dad adds. "Blunt object to the head, chloroform, and the knife." We

DRASTIC CRIMES CALL FOR DRASTIC INSIGHTS

filled him in on my vision on the way to the office. He looks expectantly at me. "We could really use your insight on this one."

Mitchell smirks, and I brace myself for the awful saying he's about to spew on the room. "Yeah, drastic crimes call for drastic insights."

"Seriously, you need to stop doing that. No one but you thinks you're funny." I roll my eyes and sip the last of my coffee.

"Not true. Marcia laughs at my jokes."

"Marcia is nice to everyone. Don't for a second think her laughter is genuine. She probably thinks she has to laugh at your pathetic jokes since you're always leaving her huge tips."

"She deserves those tips. I've seen the way she takes care of you." There's an implied "Lord knows you can't take care of yourself" attached to Mitchell's comment.

"If you two are finished, can we focus on the case, please?" Dad huffs and shuffles through the files on his desk, which is plenty big enough to display about ten case files and still have room for his laptop. Not that I'm bitter or anything that he takes up more of my office than I do when I'm the one who started the PI business.

"There has to be a reason why these women in particular were targeted," Dad continues. "What aren't we seeing?" He lays three pictures out in a row.

"Maybe he just hates women," Mitchell says.

I glare at him. "That's your answer? They're all women, so he hates women in general?"

"Why is it always two steps forward, three steps back with you? I thought we were past the bitterness and actually on friendly terms." Mitchell crosses his arms in front of his chest.

"Are we here to discuss our feelings or solve a case? You should know me by now. If you're failing at your job, I'm going to call you out on it because what you do affects my reputation." And Lord knows I've struggled to keep a positive reputation. Most people look at me as a hack. They think I'm good at using deductive reasoning and pretend to have these psychic abilities. Even after they witness me reading objects.

"Piper," Dad says, "where is all this anger coming from? This isn't like you."

"Yeah, I'm used to your sarcasm, but you're bordering on..."

I wag a finger at him. "I dare you to say 'bitchy.' Go ahead. See what will happen."

"See. *That*. What is up with you?" Mitchell asks, getting up and walking across the office as if he doesn't want to be near me.

I look at Dad. "I don't know. I've felt weird ever since I had that vision at the park. Angry. Really angry."

"Are you channeling the kidnapper?" Dad asks.

"It's possible I guess. But if the vision was from Sky's perspective, why would the kidnapper's emotions be affecting me?" It doesn't add up.

"Why don't you tell us more about the vision itself? What exactly did you see?" Dad places his hand on top of mine on my desk.

I take a deep breath, not allowing myself to get upset that Dad is coddling me when he knows I hate that. "Sky was washing her hands and thinking about some girl named Tamara."

Mitchell walks over and whips out his pad and pen to take notes. "Tamara. Did she have a last name?"

"Do you often think about people and refer to them by their full names?" I snap.

Mitchell points the cap end of the pen at me. "I know you're channeling the kidnapper's anger, so I'm going to let that slide. Go on."

"Sky was upset that this Tamara person got an office job straight out of college while Sky is left to walk dogs for money."

"We can look into where Sky went to school and find out who was in her graduating class. Tamara isn't that common of a name, so we might be able to track her down."

"No need. Tamara isn't important to the case."

Mitchell looks up from his notepad. "What makes you say that?"

"I just know. Tamara is only important as far as Sky being angry because of her."

"So maybe it is Sky's emotions you're tapping into," Dad says, squeezing my hand.

No. I know it's not. "Her feelings for Tamara go beyond anger. She's..."

"Jealous," Mitchell offers. "Her friend landed the job Sky wanted, and Sky feels inadequate because of it."

That's it. "Jealousy." I nod. "But Sky doesn't feel inadequate. She legitimately felt that job should have been hers. I get the sense they both interviewed for the position."

"Okay, but what does this have to do with why Sky would be kidnapped?" Mitchell puts the pad and pen down on my desk. "You're focused on this, so it has to mean something."

My visions always mean something, but they can be so damn cryptic.

"Let's go back to looking at all three women together," Dad says. He displays the three pictures across his desk. He taps Maggie's first. "What stands out to you about the visions you had concerning Maggie?"

I reach over and place my hand on her image. "The kidnapper put an apple in her lunch bag and asked if he could tempt her."

Mitchell holds up a finger. "There was the decaying pomegranate in Carmen's car."

"And in my vision, the kidnapper said the 'aged forbidden fruit' was still tempting." My gaze volleys between Carmen's and Maggie's pictures.

"Could this guy be targeting women who rejected him?" Mitchell asks. "That could be why he didn't let any of them see him when he attacked them."

"That does make sense," Dad says, "but what about Sky? You didn't find any fruit at the park, did you?"

I slam my hand against my forehead. "How could I be so stupid? I didn't even think to look, yet I've questioned the fruit being important all along." I get up, grabbing my jacket from the back of my chair. "Let's go. We need to get back to that park and check for fruit in the restroom."

Mitchell stands up, but he shakes his head. "The entire park looked like it had just been cleaned. I doubt the trash would still be there if that's what you're thinking."

"You're right. Damn it. That bathroom was cleaned before we got there this morning." A thought pops into my head. "If only we knew who found the dogs and untied them from the water fountain."

"Does the change in topic mean you don't think any fruit was left in the restroom?" Mitchell asks, slipping into his jacket.

As soon as he poses the question, I know the answer. "My senses say no."

"Okay, why don't you two head back to the park? See if

any maintenance people are around and if any of them remember cleaning up fruit in or around the restroom," Dad suggests. "See if anyone saw who untied the dogs, too. I'll keep trying to find a connection between the three women."

"Good thinking, Dad." I wave to him before heading out.

Mitchell breaks just about every traffic law to get to the park. Time isn't on our side, though. This kidnapper is abducting women at an alarming rate. Sky could be dead by this time tomorrow and that would free the kidnapper up to take another woman.

Or man.

"That's weird," I say as we pull into the park.

"What is?" Mitchell looks around, assuming I saw something.

"I just had a thought pop into my head. The kidnapper has been focused on women, but that's going to change."

Mitchell cuts the engine and turns to face me. "Did you foresee the future?" If he widens his eyes anymore, they might pop right out of his head.

"No. I don't think so. The kidnapper must have already decided who his next victim is, and it's a man."

"Does that mean Sky and the other women are dead?"

A sinking feeling in my gut tells me if they aren't already, they will be soon. "We need to move. Quickly."

We get out of the car and head for the restrooms. There are plenty of people at the park now, which isn't going to make this easier. I look around for signs of maintenance staff, but don't see any. There's a group of mothers with their children in the pavilion attached to the restrooms, so I decide to approach them and see if any of them were here yesterday when Sky disappeared.

Mitchell doesn't ask what my plan is. He just lets me take the lead.

"Excuse me," I say when we approach the table of women. They stop talking and look up at me. "Hi, I'm Piper Ashwell. I'm a private investigator. And this is Detective Brennan." I motion to Mitchell. "We're investigating a missing persons case and were wondering if any of you were here during the day yesterday."

"Are you saying someone went missing from *this* park?" The brunette woman at the far end of the table jabs her index finger into the tabletop.

"Unfortunately, yes." A few moms stand up and start gathering their things. I should have thought about how to best phrase this so I didn't start a mass panic. "You're all in a group, which is a good thing. The woman who was abducted was alone in the restroom at the time."

"It was a woman? Not a child?" a redhead near Mitchell asks.

"That's correct."

"Do you know why she was taken?" the redhead adds.

"No, we don't. But we're fairly certain the kidnapper is targeting adults, not children."

"Fairly certain isn't good enough for me." The brunette at the other end of the table flings her diaper bag over her shoulder and walks to the sandbox to collect her son. I can't blame her. I guess I'd react the same way if I had a child. Not that I'll ever find out.

"Were you here yesterday?" Mitchell asks the redhead.

She nods. "With both of my boys. I homeschool my oldest son. He's right over there." She points to the swings where a boy about nine years old is sitting but not swinging. "He doesn't like coming here. Says it's too babyish for him.

He was excited yesterday when all the dogs were here, though."

The kid who freed the dogs. "Ma'am, did your son untie those dogs by any chance?"

Her face turns almost as red as her hair. "He's a handful. I was distracted by my toddler, Freddie, and Jack slipped by me. I think he wanted to walk the dogs. He's always asking for one, but my husband is allergic."

"Do you think I could talk to Jack?" I ask. "I promise I'll make it quick, and I don't have to tell him it's for a police investigation. I don't want to scare him."

"He'd probably think it was cool. He wants to be a police officer when he grows up."

This is great. "Is that a yes, then?"

She nods and walks us over to Jack. "Jack, this is..." She pauses, having forgotten our names.

"Piper Ashwell, private investigator, and Detective Brennan with the Weltunkin PD," I say.

Jack hops off the swing. "Cool." His face lights up, but then he suddenly looks worried. "Am I in trouble for letting those dogs loose? Are you going to arrest me?"

Mitchell bends down to Jack. "Not at all, champ. In fact, you might be able to help us crack a case. Would you like to try?"

Jack smiles and does a perfect impression of a bobble head doll.

"Great." Mitchell ruffles his hair.

"Jack, did you see any fruit in the pavilion yesterday?" I ask.

"Fruit? I thought we were talking about the dogs."

"We are, but we think someone left some fruit behind, too. Do you remember seeing any?"

Jack shakes his head. "There was an onion, though.

Right on top of the water fountain. I thought that was weird, especially since it didn't smell like an onion."

"An onion?" Mitchell asks. "Are you sure?"

"I think it was a red onion. Mom puts them in our salads. I don't like them."

An onion wouldn't make sense. I wrack my brain for a fruit that looks like a red onion, and snap my fingers when the answer comes to me. "Could it have been a fig?"

"A what?" Jack asks.

"He's never had one, so he wouldn't know," his mother says before rushing over to the sandpit to grab her toddler, who is trying to crawl out of the contained area.

"Did you notice the dogs barking at all?" Mitchell asks.

"Yeah, that's how I found them. I was over there on the other side of the pavilion. I heard the barking and came to see what it was about."

"Did you see anyone with the dogs?" I ask.

"No, but they were all turned in the same direction and barking, so I guess whoever made them bark had already left before I got there."

So the kidnapper put the fig in the water fountain and then took Sky. The dogs were probably barking at both the kidnapper and Sky, since Sky left them.

"Thank you, Jack. You've been a big help."

After thanking the mother too, Mitchell and I start for his Explorer.

"What do apples, figs, and pomegranates have in common other than being fruits?" he asks me.

"Forbidden fruits," I blurt out without thinking. "There all types of forbidden fruits according to the Bible and Greek mythology."

"Really? A fig? I don't remember that from church."

"Adam and Eve made clothing from fig leaves after they

ate from the tree of knowledge and realized they were naked." I stop walking and grab Mitchell's arm.

"What is it?"

"This is all just coming to me. Don't you see?"

"See what?"

"Church. This is all stuff you learn about in church. That's the connection between the three women. They all attend the same church."

"You think the kidnapper is someone from their church?"

I nod, equally as horrified by the revelation as Mitchell is.

CHAPTER FOURTEEN

While Mitchell drives, I call Dad. He picks up on the second ring. "Maggie, Carmen, and Sky all attend the same church. We need to find out which one that is." My mind goes back to the basket I found on Carmen's front porch. It was from someone named Emily who was in charge of the Sunday school. "The person heading up the Sunday school is named Emily," I add, and Mitchell nods his understanding.

"I'm on it. Where are you two now?"

"Driving to the first church I find," Mitchell says.

"I'm searching Carmen's and Emily's names along with Sunday school in Weltunkin. Give me a second." I hear the keys clicking on Dad's laptop. "Bingo! Weltunkin House of God. It's the big church on Hamilton Street, and the minister is a man named Pastor Evans."

Mitchell puts his portable police light on the roof and makes a U-turn at the next intersection. "On our way."

"Dad, I need a list of all church members, employees, whatever you can find," I say.

"I'll see what I can do. And you two be careful. I know

churches are supposed to be sacred places, but if the kidnapper is connected to the church, you could be in danger going there."

"We will, Dad." I disconnect the call.

"Anything else coming to you?" Mitchell asks, knowing the more I start to unravel a case, the more truths reveal themselves.

"Nothing yet." I twist the ring on my pinky finger. "Believe me, I wish my brain would finish connecting all the dots."

"I never would have connected the fruit to the church," Mitchell says. "Or thought the 'red onion' Jack mentioned was a fig. You're doing great, Piper."

Hearing people say that when I'm struggling to see more never makes me feel better, but I know Mitchell means well.

We pull into the church parking lot as the bell in the clock tower chimes noon.

"Can I confess something?" Mitchell asks, cutting the engine and turning toward me.

"Sure." I unclick my seat belt.

"Churches make me very uncomfortable, like I'm being judged."

Ah. His history with women must be why he's hesitant to be judged.

"We've all sinned if that's what you're worried about." My head twinges with a familiar buzzing. Something about what I just said is important to this case.

"Do you have a headache?" Mitchell motions to my hand, which is pressed against my right temple.

"We've all sinned," I repeat, and the twinge comes again. "The killer is targeting people who sin."

"Killer? When did you start thinking the kidnapper is actually a killer, too?"

A while ago, but now I'm convinced of it. "He's targeting sinners." Something is still off. *Forbidden fruit. Sinners.* What am I missing? "Ugh."

"Piper, take it easy. You can't force this. Let's go inside and talk to the minister." He places his hand on my shoulder and looks directly into my eyes.

"Okay," I say, no longer pushing against my temple.

The church is huge. There are several rooms for worship, and one hallway is full of classrooms. I'd guess for preschool and Sunday school. We walk around until we find a door with a nameplate that reads: *Pastor Evans.*

Mitchell knocks.

"Come in," calls a deep male voice.

Mitchell opens the door, and we walk in to find a bald man smiling at us from his desk chair.

"Please come sit. How can I help you both today?"

Knowing churches make Mitchell uncomfortable, I start talking. "Pastor Evans, I'm Piper, and this is Mitchell." I don't want to alert him to our professions just yet, but at the same time, I get a pang of guilt for withholding information from a religious figure. "We wanted to talk to you because three women who attend this church have gone missing."

Pastor Evans's smile quickly disappears. "Three women, you say?" He holds up a finger and closes his eyes. "I thought it was odd that Carmen was not at services this past Sunday. Is she one of them?"

"Yes. So are Maggie Burns and Sky Lucas."

"Sky." Pastor Evans shakes his head, his gaze back on Mitchell and me. "I pray for that girl. She's bright and has so much potential, but her constant envy of those around her holds her back."

Envy.

"And Carmen, she devotes a lot of time to our children here, but she isn't as good with the adults. I've had some complaints that she is always boasting of her accomplishments. I warned her pride is something to be wary of exhibiting."

Pride.

"What about Maggie?" I ask.

Pastor Evans leans forward on his desk. "I'm afraid I can not disclose what Maggie has confided in me."

I'm sure he's referring to her infidelity.

Lust.

Envy. Pride. Lust. Envy. Pride. Lust.

"The seven deadly sins," I blurt out.

"No, she's not guilty of all of them. That would be excessive. But as I tell the members of the church, no person is perfect. None of us is God, right? I'm sure if we all engage in self-reflection, we'll see we are guilty of at least one of the seven deadly sins."

"Do you talk about the seven deadly sins a lot during your services?" I ask, and I can feel Mitchell's eyes on me.

"Perhaps not enough, but I've been told I can harp on a subject." He gives a brief chuckle before his expression turns grave once again. "I take it you two are detectives. Am I correct?"

"I am," Mitchell says, raising his hand as if we're in school.

"I'm a private investigator," I say, not willing to tell a religious man that I have abilities that go beyond what his beliefs say mere humans should be capable of.

"I see. Do you have any leads on who might have harmed my three church members?"

I clear my throat, knowing he's not going to like this.

"We do. You see, the only thing these three women have in common is that they are members of this church."

Mitchell's body tenses in my peripheral vision. He must think I'm about to accuse Pastor Evans. I'm not at all, and I have to get him off that train of thought before he does something rash—like handcuff the poor minister.

"I believe their kidnapper is also a member of this church. It's the only reason why he would know all three women since their paths don't cross anywhere else."

"I see." Pastor Evans leans back in his chair. "I can't tell you how deeply this hurts my heart. How can I assist you both in finding this person?"

A knock on the door draws our attention.

"Excuse me one moment," Pastor Evans says to us before calling out, "Come in."

An overweight man in a gray janitor's uniform enters the office. "Pastor, I finished emptying all the garbage cans. Is it okay if I take my lunch break now?"

"Yes, Lester. Thank you. And after lunch, can you please see about getting fresh flowers for the worship halls?"

Lester visibly slumps. "We're low on fresh flowers outside. They had to be dug up for the cemetery work being done."

"I understand. Well, try to see what you can come up with."

Lester nods, but it's accompanied by a sigh as he leaves the room and closes the door behind him.

"I'm sorry about that. Lester is not the best worker, but he needs direction and purpose, and I'm happy this church can provide that for him."

Another knock sounds on the door. Apparently, lunchtime is busy around here.

DRASTIC CRIMES CALL FOR DRASTIC INSIGHTS

Pastor Evans gives us a "what can you do?" expression before calling, "Come in."

"Pastor, we're in the process of contacting the last family for permission to exhume a grave."

Exhume a grave? Why are they moving bodies in the cemetery?

"Good. Let me know if you need me to make any calls. I'm happy to help."

"We're all good. The night guy works really fast, so the moving process is going surprisingly well."

"I'm happy to hear it," Pastor Evans says with a nod, and the man leaves.

"You're exhuming bodies from the cemetery?" I ask.

"Unfortunately, we experienced several sinkholes that were compromising the cemetery. People were unable to visit their loved ones' graves because it was unsafe. So we got permission to move the graves. The process is going well, as you've just heard."

Mitchell looks queasy at the entire idea.

The minister sits forward in his seat. "Now, back to Maggie, Carmen, and Sky. How can I help you?"

"We need to know if there's a man who talks to all three of them here at church. Possibly someone who might have been interested in romantic relationships with them," I add.

"Romantic relationships? Maggie is a married woman, so I'd hope none of the members of my church would pursue her in that manner." He taps his finger on the top of his desk, making me wonder if he's considering it could be true.

"I know Maggie was having an affair," I say.

"Are you friends with her?" Pastor Evans asks.

"No. We discovered the affair through a mutual friend

of the man she was seeing." *Friend* is stretching it, but I'm trying not to freak out the damn minister.

"I see."

"We are also under the impression that Maggie was having more than one affair."

Lust.

"Yeah, yeah, stupid senses. I get it already! She was a sinner!"

"Piper?" Mitchell places his hand on my arm.

"Oh, God. Did I just say that out loud?"

Mitchell nods.

I cover my mouth, realizing I just took the Lord's name in vain inside a church with a minister present. "I'm so sorry."

"What senses were you referring to?" Pastor Evans asks, his hands steepled on the desk in front of him.

Just wonderful. If I keep this up, I may find myself the recipient of an exorcism before I make it out of the church.

I stand up. "Pastor, we've taken up enough of your time, and I'm sure you're hungry for lunch, so we'll get out of your hair." I cringe, and my gaze is drawn to his bald head.

"That would be rather difficult to do considering I don't have any," Pastor Evans says with a smile. At least he has a sense of humor.

"I am so sorry. I clearly need some rest." I start for the door with Mitchell a half step behind me, just as eager to get out of here.

"If I think of anything that might be helpful, should I call the Weltunkin PD?" Pastor Evans calls after us.

"Oh." Mitchell turns around and grabs a card from inside his jacket. "Here you go. Thank you for your time." He flees as quickly as possible, and I close the door behind him.

DRASTIC CRIMES CALL FOR DRASTIC INSIGHTS

"Wow, you were worse than I was," he says as we walk out of the church.

"I can't believe I said those things." As we exit the building, my eyes go to the cemetery positioned to the left in the back of the church parking lot. I'm not sure how I didn't notice the machinery when we arrived, but I guess I was too focused on talking to the minister.

"Something wrong?" Mitchell asks, following my gaze.

"I don't know. It's just odd to move graves. What happened to resting in peace? It seems wrong and gives me this creeped out feeling."

"They're digging up graves. That's enough to unnerve anyone." Mitchell shudders.

It's something else, though. Dead bodies aren't scary. They can't hurt you because they're dead. So why am I so freaked out by that cemetery?

CHAPTER FIFTEEN

"Does this guy think he's punishing people for their sins or something?" Mitchell asks back at the office, where we are having a late lunch with Dad.

I unwrap my Italian hero from Matty's Sub Shop and take a large bite as I contemplate Mitchell's question. It feels right that this person connected to the church is trying to rid the world of what he deems to be the worst sinners. I slowly nod my head.

"One point for Junior," Dad says, making me laugh and nearly choke on my food.

"Hey," Mitchell whines. "I'm used to Piper taking jabs at me, but now you're doing it, too?"

Dad winks at me as he bites into his roast beef and Swiss. Is he picking on Mitchell in an attempt to stop me from doing it? Beating me to the punch? I'm not really liking the role reversal where I feel the need to referee.

"How was Jez when you checked on her?" I ask Dad, trying to change the topic all together.

"Fine. She's such a sweet dog. Not like Max. He can be such a terror."

Max is the only dog I've encountered who isn't happy with my abilities because I always know when he's up to no good.

"I feel bad that I'm away so much. She must get so bored."

"You can always drop her off at my place," Dad says. "She might teach Max how to behave."

"Or Max might ruin Jezebel," Mitchell says.

"Not possible. Jez is a good girl." I really lucked out with her. And I don't sense that she misses her former owner either. She's just as happy with me as I am with her.

Mitchell finishes his sub and balls up the paper it was wrapped in. "Alright, back to this case. We have three missing women, and Piper believes the next victim will be a man. So, do we check out the list of church members?"

Dad reaches for a piece of paper to the right of his laptop. "There's no official list of members. But I did find programs from different performances the church has put on, so it lists quite a few people, especially those in the church choir." He hands the paper to me.

I put my sandwich down, wipe my hands on a napkin, and take a deep breath before taking it from him. Then I close my eyes and focus on clearing my mind. Once I'm satisfied, I open my eyes and begin scanning the list. Usually a name jumps out at me. It either looks bold or bigger than the others, and that's how I know it's the one I'm looking for. But as I scan the list, nothing is sticking out to me. I slowly read each name in my head, hoping that will trigger something, but I'm left with one conclusion.

"The person we're looking for isn't on this." I put the paper down. "I have to be missing something. We were at that church. I should have sensed something."

Dad places his hand on my shoulder. "Pumpkin, we've

talked about this. You can't put so much pressure on yourself. Mitchell and I are working this case, too. It's not all on you."

Except Mitchell and Dad don't have my abilities. They can only question people and look for clues. I have to see what they can't. Otherwise, I'm not a help to them at all.

"Stop it," Mitchell says, giving me a judgmental stare. "I know what you're thinking, and you're wrong."

I pick up a pen on my desk and begin turning it end over end in my hand, mostly to avoid having to look at Mitchell.

"Let's go back to the basics and look at our clues," Dad says.

I don't want to rehash what we already know. I want to have a vision. One that will actually lead me to the killer.

"Whoa." I sit back in my desk chair and drop the pen.

"What is it?" Mitchell leans forward in the seat across from me. "Did you see something?"

"I just thought of the guy as a killer again, and the thought felt like a definite truth."

"Are you saying Maggie and Carmen are dead?" Dad asks.

I let the question float around in my mind before answering. "Yes. And Sky, too. They're all dead." My breathing increases. These people are dead because I couldn't solve this case in time. Every person I fail to save stays with me. I never forget them. I see their faces in my sleep. I'm thankful I'm not a medium, because I'd probably see their spirits around me all the time, angry with me for not saving them, asking me why I spent my time having family dinners when I should have been out searching for them. I push the chair away from my desk and stand up.

"I shouldn't be sitting around. I need to get back to that

DRASTIC CRIMES CALL FOR DRASTIC INSIGHTS

church and figure out who is doing this. I can't let him take anyone else. I can't let anyone else die because of—"

Mitchell is around my desk with his hands gripping my arms before I can finish. He looks deep into my eyes. "None of this is because of you. Do you hear me?" His tone is forceful. "None of it. Without you, we wouldn't know the killer was connected to the church. Without you, we wouldn't have picked up on the forbidden fruit clues. Without you, we'd be sitting here twiddling our thumbs."

"He's right, pumpkin. We can't save everyone. It's the sad truth. We're human. We do our best, but we lose a lot of good people in the process." Dad's on his feet now, too.

"I have to do something. I need to go to that church and sit in every pew if I have to until I get a read on this guy." Since the next service isn't until Sunday, this is my only option. I can't sit around for days as the body count continues to pile up.

"Then let's go," Mitchell says.

Dad nods. "I'll go with you."

Pastor Evans is in a meeting when we arrive, so we head to the fellowship hall. The room is big with red carpeting and a high ceiling. Sitting in every pew is going to take a while, so I decide to get right to it and not waste any time. I choose the first one on my right. Dad and Mitchell walk up the aisle. I'm not sure what they're looking for, but I understand neither wants to stand around with their hands in their pockets while I do my thing.

I give each spot a few seconds before sliding to the next. I make sure to touch everything with my right hand, which becomes unpleasant when I spot something on the seat that could either be a dried food particle or something a young kid dug out of their nose. I get as close to it as I dare but don't touch it. *Where is the cleaning crew?*

It takes me two hours to touch everything in the room, and my fingertips feel numb from running my hand over all the surfaces. I open and close my fingers a few times to work out the kinks in my joints, and then I sigh so loudly both Dad and Mitchell look up at me.

"I don't understand it. I know he's part of this church, but I can't sense him anywhere."

Mitchell looks up at the podium. "What if you aren't sensing him in the pews because he doesn't sit there."

Ding, ding, ding!

"He doesn't," I say.

"Wait." Dad walks over to me. "Are you saying you think Pastor Evans is the killer?"

"Only one way to find out." I step up to the podium and look out across the hall, imagining how Pastor Evans sees his constituents in this room at every service. Dad and Mitchell flank my sides.

"We're right here," Mitchell says, sensing my hesitation.

It's not that I'm overly religious, but if the killer turns out to be the head of the church... What will that do to this town?

I slowly raise my right hand and place it on top of the podium.

Pastor Evans looks out at the crowd seated before him. "So many sins and they don't even realize it. Or they don't care. Why do they think coming here every Sunday makes up for how they live their lives the other six days of the week? Don't they hear my sermons? Don't they know God is always watching them? I don't know how else to get through to them. As much as I hate to do this, it's the only way."

DRASTIC CRIMES CALL FOR DRASTIC INSIGHTS

When the vision ends, I nearly fall over, but Mitchell is there to steady me on my feet.

"What is it? Did you see the killer?"

Goose bumps cover my arms and legs under my clothing, despite the heat being cranked in the church. "I heard his thoughts." I swallow the lump in my throat. "I was him in the vision."

"The killer?" Mitchell asks.

It seemed that way, but I don't want to believe it. I don't want it to be true. Still, I know what I have to do. I have to confront Pastor Evans. I have to tell him about my psychic abilities and what I just saw. And then I need to read him, even if it's by force.

CHAPTER SIXTEEN

"Piper?" Dad asks, placing his hand on the small of my back. "Say something."

"I saw Pastor Evans."

Dad's hand drops, and Mitchell's eyes widen. I know they both thought I saw the killer in the crowd, not that I was implicating Pastor Evans.

"We need to talk to him right now." I start for the door with Dad and Mitchell on my heels.

"Are you sure about this?" Mitchell asks. "I mean, he's a minister. This can't be right."

"Her visions are never wrong," Dad says. "Piper, what exactly did you see?"

"It was what I heard, and I think it's best if you find out when I reveal it to Pastor Evans himself." More like I can't go through this twice. I march right up to the minister's door and knock loudly, wondering how I didn't sense anything off about him when I met him.

"Come in," comes his friendly voice, though there's something different about it today. It's almost sad. Does he not want to kill these people but feels he has to? I shake the thought from my head as I open the door and step inside.

Pastor Evans looks up from his desk at us and removes his reading glasses. "Miss Ashwell, Detective Brennan..." His gaze goes to Dad, who steps forward with his hand outstretched.

"Detective Thomas Ashwell."

"Pleasure to meet you. I must say I'm both nervous and relieved to see another detective on this case." Pastor Evans's gaze volleys between us, and then he motions for us to sit. "I'll grab another chair." He starts to stand, but Mitchell holds up his hand to stop him.

"I'm fine to stand."

Pastor Evans nods and sits down again. "Very well. What can I do for you?"

Here goes nothing. "Pastor, I'm afraid I withheld some information from you the last time I was here."

"Oh?" He tilts his head as if trying to read my mind. "Well, I've been told I'm a good listener, so please proceed whenever you're ready."

Does he think I'm going to confess my sins or something? "I'm not your everyday private investigator. I'm..." I look down at my hands in my lap. "I'm psychic."

"I see." His tone is unexpectedly nonjudgmental. "God has bestowed you with a gift."

"You believe me then?" I meet his gaze.

"I have no reason to believe you'd lie to me." He waves his hand, gesturing that I should continue.

"Well, I was just in your fellowship hall, and I had a vision."

"Do you see the future, Ms. Ashwell?" Now he sounds skeptical.

"No. I see the past and present."

He nods. "Ah. I'm happy to hear that. While I'm open-minded, I do believe only God himself can see what has not yet happened."

"I saw you, Pastor."

He doesn't look fazed.

"Or more like I heard your thoughts. You were looking out over your constituents and were displeased that they all sinned so much. You thought, and I quote, 'I don't know how else to get through to them. As much as I hate to do this, it's the only way.'" I hear Mitchell's intake of air behind me. "Can you please explain to us what you meant by that?"

Pastor Evans steeples his hands in front of him on the desk. "I can see how you might misinterpret that. And I must say, it is impressive that you know the exact wording of my thoughts. You definitely have been blessed with a gift from God, Ms. Ashwell."

Why won't he just answer the question already? Is he stalling for time to come up with a way to twist his own words to be less incriminating? I drum my fingers against my thigh, trying to remain patient with the man.

Dad clears his throat and adjusts his tie. "My daughter is definitely gifted, Pastor, and quite frankly, she's our best chance at finding out what is going on at your church."

"I have to disagree with you there, Detective. God is our best chance, but if he's choosing to act through your daughter, so be it."

I don't care what he believes. I just need to read him. "Pastor, may I show you what I can do?" I lean forward in my seat so I'm able to reach for his hand if he allows it.

"I believe you've already shown me, Ms. Ashwell. And as for your previous question, I was making the decision to give a very difficult talk to my members. So many of them struggle with sins they need to learn to avoid. Temptation can be a daily evil we battle with."

Temptation. The killer wondered if he could tempt Maggie. I look to Mitchell, who appears to be thinking the same thing. Pastor Evans could be our man. I scoot forward even more in my seat and place my hand on top of Pastor Evans's under the guise of an understanding gesture. "I'm sure you do all you can for them, Pastor." I give his hand a small squeeze as he smiles. Then I close my eyes.

"I understand this is a sensitive subject, Monique, but your uncle's grave could be affected by this sinkhole if we don't do something now to stop it. No one likes having to move the remains of a loved one once they are at peace, but I ask you to remember that your uncle's body is just that now. His soul is in Heaven. I assure you this process will not disturb him in any way."

The woman sitting across from him dabs her eyes with a tissue and nods. "I know, Pastor. It's just that he was like a father to me. He raised me after my parents were killed in a car accident. He was a good man, and I don't want to do anything to disturb—" A sob chokes her words, and the minister gets up and walks around his desk to sit in the chair beside her. He takes her hand in his.

"My dear, moving his remains so you can continue to visit his grave is the best scenario. I assure you we will handle his remains with the utmost care and respect. My crew is being extremely careful."

Pastor Evans's hand slides out from under mine, and when I open my eyes, he has his head cocked. "May I ask what that was about?"

"She was praying for you and your church," Mitchell offers. "Weren't you, Piper?"

Why not? It will freak him out a lot less than the truth.

"I'm sorry, Pastor. Sometimes the urge to pray overwhelms me."

He leans back in his seat and crosses his hands on top of his stomach, which is slightly rounded in the center. "I of all people understand the need for prayer. Thank you for praying for my church and its people."

"Pastor, would we be able to talk to some of your members?" I ask.

"That would be up to them. I can't speak for anyone but myself. You are certainly welcome to attend our service on Sunday. It begins at 10:00 a.m."

I can't wait until Sunday. Too many people could be dead and buried by then. "Thank you. We look forward to it," I say, standing up.

Mitchell and Dad have no idea what my plan is, but they get up as well. Mitchell grabs my elbow as we walk toward the car. "What's going on? What did you see?"

"Nothing helpful. He was talking to someone about moving her uncle's grave."

Dad stops walking. "Then we should check out the cemetery."

"Afraid that's not possible," says a man with a shovel walking toward us from the cemetery. He wipes sweat from his brow with the back of his gloved hand. "It's not safe to be anywhere near the cemetery right now with all the sinkholes. The church members with family buried there aren't happy in the least, but no one expected this to happen. Apparently, there's an underground stream eroding the land and causing all the problems. We're trying to move the graves quickly enough to stop anyone's final resting place from being destroyed."

"That's very unfortunate," Dad says, extending his

DRASTIC CRIMES CALL FOR DRASTIC INSIGHTS

hand. "I'm Detective Thomas Ashwell. This is Detective Brennan and my daughter, Piper Ashwell."

Mitchell steps forward to shake hands with the man, setting me up to do the same, but with my usual twist. I notice the watch peeking out from between the man's gloved hand and his sleeve, so when I shake his hand, I hold on and say, "That's a beautiful watch you have. Was it a gift?" I don't hear his response.

"We're moving as quickly as we can, Pastor. We could really use some more men on the job, though."

"I've hired another man for the night crew. He's one of the church members. He's a good worker, so I think he'll be a big help to you."

"We could certainly use it."

"Ms.?" The man pulls his hand from mine.

"I'm sorry. I haven't gotten much sleep lately, and I guess I zoned out for a moment. It's just that your watch reminded me of one my grandfather used to wear." I clear my throat and step back so my arm nudges Dad without being obvious to anyone but him.

"Oh, yes," Dad says. "Look at that. It does look like Grandpa Bill's watch."

"We won't hold you up any longer," I say, giving the man a small wave.

We don't talk until we get back to Mitchell's Explorer. Mitchell doesn't start the engine. Instead, he clicks his seat belt and turns to face me in the back seat since Dad is riding shotgun.

"Nothing but dead ends. I kept seeing things revolving around the cemetery, but that's it. It could be my senses trying to tell me the missing women are already dead." I twist the ring on my pinky.

"Or maybe the people being taken are related to the

people whose graves are being moved," Mitchell says, shocking the hell out of me.

"Piper?" Dad asks. "Does that sound right to you? You're gawking at Mitchell."

"I just can't believe I didn't think of that. In my latest vision, I saw a woman named Monique. Maybe we should find her to make sure she's okay."

"But you said the next victim would be male," Mitchell says.

I shake my head. "I don't know for sure that the next victim will be. I'm just sensing that one of them will be a male." Unfortunately, that could mean the one I'm going to actually find before it's too late will be a male. "We need to find this Monique woman and go see her now."

Dad unclicks his seat belt. "I'll go." He opens his door and steps out without any protest from Mitchell or me.

Mitchell leans his head back on the headrest. "Talk to me. Let's think this through out loud."

I rub my forehead, willing my brain to make sense of all this. "We're not going to save most of these victims, if any."

Mitchell's head jerks up. "What makes you say that?"

"I just feel it." I press my hand to my stomach, which is lurching with the undeniable proof that I'm failing. "That cemetery is going to be filled with quite a few more bodies." The statement comes to me as an absolute truth. As much as I try to desensitize myself to this aspect of my job, it never gets any easier. Why do I have this ability if I can't save everyone I see in my visions? What's the point of it besides torturing me?

"I'm sorry. I know this must be harder on you than any other detective or PI. You get more emotionally invested thanks to your visions. I don't know how I'd deal with that if I were in your shoes."

"I don't have a choice. It's not like I can ignore my visions."

"No, but you seek them out. You choose to become involved in these cases, and maybe I'm to blame for that."

I look at him through the rearview mirror. "I got involved in this long before my father became your partner. I've been solving cases since I was twelve. You've only been at this for a few years. You might be older than I am, but I've put in more time than you have."

"I'm only two years older than you, so why do you treat me like I'm an old man?" He smirks at me in the mirror. "Is it to avoid throwing yourself at me? A defense mechanism?"

I roll my eyes. "Keep dreaming, Grandpa."

He laughs, and Dad returns with a piece of paper in hand.

"Took some convincing since Pastor Evans believes in the privacy of his members, but when I told him she could be the next victim if he didn't cooperate, he changed his attitude."

"Did you tell him about my vision?" I sit forward in the seat.

"No. I just told him our theory is that the victims might be related to the people whose graves have been affected by the sinkholes. He actually put a pretty big damper on that theory by letting me know Maggie doesn't have any relatives buried in the cemetery at all, in the part affected by the sinkholes or not."

"So do we still look into this Monique woman?" Mitchell asks, his gaze on me.

"I must have seen her for a reason," I say.

"Then we'll go." Mitchell starts the engine, and Dad types the address into his phone's navigation.

When we arrive at Monique Dubois's house on

Millington Way, my jaw nearly drops to my lap. I've dealt with truly wealthy people before, but Monique's house looks like something you'd see in a magazine featuring celebrity homes. And one word rings through my mind: *Greed.*

CHAPTER SEVENTEEN

Mitchell and Dad are standing outside the car, but I'm still in my seat. Dad opens my door.

"You coming, pumpkin?"

"Greed. Monique is the epitome of greed." I undo my seat belt and slide out of the seat as I stare up at the mansion with the six-car garage. There's a lagoon out front with a bridge and a wishing well. The ground is so perfectly landscaped you could probably play golf on it if it weren't too cold right now.

"I have to agree with you there," Mitchell says, eyeing up the property. "That certainly makes Monique fit the description of one of the killer's targets."

We walk up to the double front doors, and Dad rings the bell. A woman answers the door, but it's not Monique.

"Can I help you?" she asks, her eyes taking us in one by one.

"We'd like to speak with Monique Dubois, please," I say since neither Dad nor Mitchell knows this isn't her. Although the woman's plain clothing is a dead giveaway if you ask me.

"I'm sorry but Ms. Dubois isn't home right now. Can I take a message for her?"

Mitchell steps forward and extends his hand while giving the woman a flirtatious smile. "I'm Detective Mitchell Brennan. My partners and I are investigating a missing persons case, and we'd like to ask Ms. Dubois a few questions. Do you happen to know when she'll be returning home?"

The woman brushes her hair behind her ear, and her cheeks pink as she stares at Mitchell. "I hope Ms. Dubois isn't in any sort of trouble."

"No. Nothing like that," Mitchell says, even though I'm pretty sure she's the next target, which makes her in a heap of trouble.

"Do you know where Ms. Dubois is?" I interrupt, pushing Mitchell aside.

"She has yoga at the country club on Wednesday evenings. After that, she usually goes out for dinner and drinks with friends."

Weltunkin Country Club. Got it.

"Thank you. You've been very helpful," I say, turning on my heel and starting back toward the car.

Dad comes with me, but Mitchell is still talking to the woman. I know he hasn't been on a date in a while, but I wish he'd hit on women on his own time—granted we've had no free time since this case began.

"I have a proposition for you," Dad says once we're in the car waiting for Mitchell.

"What's that?"

"You two drop me off at the office so I can get my car. Then I'll go walk Jezebel for you and head home afterward while you and Mitchell go to the country club."

"Deal." Dad made it clear when he came onboard as my

partner that he didn't want to be running around at all hours of the day and night. There's no reason for all three of us to go talk to Monique, and Jezebel does need to be let out, so this is the perfect solution.

Mitchell gets in the car with a huge smile on his face. "Erica is quite the talkative one."

"Erica?" I ask, although I'm not surprised he's on a first-name basis with Monique's cleaning lady or whatever she is.

Mitchell bobs a shoulder. "We needed information. I got it. Anyway, Monique has to have the best of everything. Her yoga classes are private sessions for just her and a few of her close friends. She only associates with people of the same..." He pauses to choose his words. "I want to say 'income status' but that sounds awkward."

"We get the point," I say. "Go on."

"The ironic thing is Monique got her money from her uncle. The one buried in the church cemetery. She's never worked a day in her life. This was his house. And she refuses to get married or have children because she doesn't want to share her money with anyone."

"I'm getting the feeling Erica isn't crazy about her boss."

"She's not. But Erica is a single mother of two and has to pay the bills somehow."

A single mother of two who has eyes for Mitchell. I don't want to discuss that though, so I say, "We're dropping my dad back at the office and going to the country club on our own, so step on it before we miss Monique."

We're all quiet on the way back to the office. I see Marcia closing up the store for the day and give her a small wave as I get out of the back seat and into the passenger seat of Mitchell's Explorer.

"I got a new book in that I think you'll love," Marcia calls to me. "I'm holding it at the register for you."

"You're the best! I'll stop in tomorrow morning."

She nods and gets in her car.

"I don't suppose you have a membership to the Weltunkin Country Club," Mitchell says, pulling back out onto the road.

I scoff. "Not even in my dreams."

"Looks like I'll be flashing my badge to get us in then."

"You always do what you have to do to get what you want."

"Hmm, I'm sensing bitterness in your tone. Are you jealous when I have to flirt with other women?"

"Hardly." I turn to look out the window, watching the buildings go by in the dim lighting from the streetlights.

"Level with me. Why do you hate my flirting so much?"

For a moment, I don't respond. Mitchell knows too much about me already, but considering I spend just about every waking moment with him, I'm not sure how to have it any other way. "There's no point in me flirting with anyone because I can't get close to people like that. I can't read romance novels or watch Hallmark movies because they just remind me of what I can't have thanks to my ability. It's not a good reminder that I can't get close to people. So, when you have women fawning all over you—"

Mitchell reaches over and places his right hand on my forearm. "I'm sorry. I never thought about it like that. I can't even imagine..." He removes his hand and lets the comment linger in the air between us.

"It's fine. I've always been this way." I force out a laugh that sounds as uncomfortable as I feel. "Maybe Pastor Evans is right. Maybe my ability is a gift from God, and I'm just doing what I was designed to do."

"I think you mean 'created' to do."

"Oh, now you're going to get all religious on me?"

"You started it with the talk about gifts from God."

I smile, more at ease with our usual banter. "Can I be honest with you about something?"

He dips his head in my direction and gives me one of his seductive smiles. "You secretly dream about not having this ability so you don't have to spend all your time and energy pretending you aren't attracted to me?"

I roll my eyes. "Oh, dear Lord! Do you hear the words coming out of your mouth?"

"There you go, being all religious on me again. You could try praying, you know."

"I pray you'll stop being so full of yourself. How's that?"

"Funny." He turns into the parking lot of the Weltunkin Country Club, which is packed for a Wednesday night. He manages to find a spot without valet parking, but it means we have to hike to the entrance.

"Think we're dressed okay?" Mitchell asks, looking down at his dress pants and button down shirt, sans tie.

"I am. You can use your badge to get around your appearance." I wink, although I'm not sure where that came from. Lord help me if Mitchell is rubbing off on me.

The doorman at the club greets us with a questioning look. "Are you members of the club?" His tone implies there's no way we could be.

Mitchell produces his badge from under his shirt. "Detective Brennan with the Weltunkin PD. It is of the utmost importance that we speak with one of your members inside immediately."

"Has this person done something illegal? That's something the club would want to know about. We don't allow our members to have indiscretions that would reflect negatively on the club."

"We think this person might be in danger," I say.

"I see." He opens the door for us. "Do you know where you're going?"

"We're here to see Monique Dubois. She's having a private yoga lesson."

"Then you'll want to head downstairs. Take the elevator on the right. There are signs once you exit the elevator."

"Thank you," Mitchell says as we walk inside.

The place is immaculate and huge. The reception desk is straight in front of us, and fresh blue towels are perched on the right-hand side of the desk. We go to the elevator, which is conveniently waiting for us.

Mitchell presses the button for the lower level. "I feel like we're descending to the basement or something."

"I'm sure it will be the nicest basement you'll ever see," I say, trying not to look at the elevator walls, which are all mirrors. Who wants to see themselves from all sides when they're all sweaty from having just worked out?

"I have no doubt."

When the doors open, we walk right up to the directory on the wall. I scan it for yoga rooms. They're all grouped in the back on the left. "This way," I say.

Only two rooms are occupied, judging by the fact that their doors are closed. Since I'm the only one who knows what Monique looks like, I peek through the windows in the doors to try to find her.

"That's odd. She's not here," I say after looking into both rooms.

"Do you think her class is over?" Mitchell asks.

"No clue."

He raps his knuckles on the door in front of us, and I watch the instructor look up before approaching the door.

"I'm sorry, but this is a private class," the woman says.

Mitchell flashes his badge. "Detective Mitchell Brennan, Weltunkin PD. Is this the class Monique Dubois usually attends?"

"Yes, it is, but I'm afraid she's not here."

"Is she using the restroom or something?" Mitchell asks.

"No. She never showed up for class this evening."

Oh no. "Did her friends know she wouldn't be attending?" I ask, already fearing the worst.

"No. They tried calling her, but she didn't answer her phone."

Yet they went on with class as usual? What kind of friends are they? "Has she done this before?"

The woman hesitates as if she doesn't want to say anything bad about Monique. "Ms. Dubois has a bit of a temper. I'm sure she had a tiff with one of the women, who doesn't want to admit it to the group, and Ms. Dubois decided to stay home this evening."

Except she isn't home. She's missing. And my senses are telling me it's because the killer knew her schedule and abducted her before she made it inside the country club.

CHAPTER EIGHTEEN

"Thank you for your time," I say, turning to leave.

"Piper." Mitchell hurries after me. "What are you doing?"

"Find out what kind of car Monique drives. We need to see if it's here."

Mitchell whips out his phone. "Okay, but I'm assuming she'd valet park."

Valet park! That's it. After taking the elevator back upstairs, we head outside to speak with the valet attendant. The doorman nods to us as we exit the building.

We have to wait a moment before the valet attendant returns to his post. "Sorry," he says. "We're short staffed tonight. I guess the new guy left."

"New guy?" I ask. Did the killer pose as a valet to abduct Monique? My senses are ringing, telling me I'm right.

"Yeah, never saw him before. He went to park some lady's car, and he never came back." He shrugs and holds out his hand. "Do you have your ticket?"

"We're not picking up a car," I say. "We actually want to know about that lady you just mentioned."

When he cocks his head, Mitchell shows him his badge. "I'm Detective Brennan, and this is private investigator Piper Ashwell. We're looking for the woman you were just talking about."

"I don't even know her name. Like I said, someone else parked her car."

"Did she go inside?" I ask, jerking my thumb over my shoulder at the club.

"Not right away at least. She was angry because she left her phone in the car and she had to go find where the other guy parked the car."

"So she followed him?"

"I guess, yeah."

"Do you know where her car was parked?"

He shakes his head. "Sorry. I was busy parking another car at the time."

A BMW pulls up, and the valet takes the keys. When he gets in the car, he says, "It was a red convertible. That's all I know."

A red convertible shouldn't be difficult to find in the parking lot. "What about the man? The valet? Can you tell us what he looked like?"

The guy huffs. "I didn't really pay attention. I see a lot of people in the course of a day." He bobs one shoulder and then pulls away to park the car.

"So we're looking for a red convertible," Mitchell says, covering his eyes with his hand to block out the sun as he scans the lot.

"This guy was in the car, so I'll be able to get a read on it." I start down the first row of cars. All of them are expensive, not that I'd know much about expensive cars. Mitchell, on the other hand, is oohing and aahing over them.

"Must be nice to be able to afford cars like these," he says, and I can tell he's resisting the urge to touch the cars as we walk past them.

I'm busy looking for a red convertible. I see a spot of red on the opposite end of the lot. "Over there." I pick up my pace to a slow jog, and Mitchell falls into step with me. The convertible has the top on it, which doesn't strike me as odd considering the time of year. Though even if it were warm enough to drive with the top down, if she treasures her belongings, she'd probably put the top up to avoid theft. I touch the top of the car and close my eyes.

"I don't understand why we have to do this now. I'm on my way to my yoga class."

"We can't do anything until you sign this paper."

"But I already gave consent to move my uncle's grave."

"Verbal consent. But we need it in writing. Pastor Evans is just trying to protect the church. It couldn't survive a lawsuit."

Monique crosses her arms. "You think I'd sue a church? I'm already rich. I don't need the little bit of money the church actually has." She scoffs, completely disgusted, but the gleam in her eyes tells a different story.

"You'd steal from a baby if it got you more of your precious money," the killer thinks while trying to keep his outward composure. "Please, Ms. Dubois. I have the paper in my car. It's just one row over. If you don't sign this... I can't afford to lose my job."

"Speaking of jobs, when did you start working here anyway?" she asks as she follows him.

"Not all of us have huge bank accounts. Weltunkin is an expensive town to live in. I take whatever jobs I can get to

pay the bills." The killer mentally adds, *"Except for this job. This one is purely for the gratification of ridding the world of sinners like you."*

"Which one is your car?" Monique asks.

"On the end over there. They don't let employees take up any of the prime parking spots. We have to park by that patch of trees."

Monique scowls when she sees the beat-up black Nissan at the edge of the lot.

The killer stops at the car. "Look, I could get in a lot of trouble for conducting other business in the parking lot. Would you mind getting in the car so no one can see this and report me? I can't afford to lose this job."

"Get in that heap of junk?" Monique crosses her arms again.

"I'll pay you a hundred bucks. I know that's not much to you, but it's what I made in tips and it's all I have on me right now. Please."

"Fine. Monique looks around the lot to make sure no one is watching, and then she opens the passenger door and slips inside as quickly as possible."

The killer smiles as he gets inside.

"Where's the money?" Monique asks.

"So much for loving your uncle who gave you everything. You disgust me, you greedy little bitch."

"Excuse me?" Monique turns, and the second she does, the killer injects her with a needle.

I open my eyes. "He took her in his car. He injected her with something to knock her out. Or kill her. I don't know."

"Did you see what he looks like?"

"No. The vision was from his perspective." My breathing is labored as the anger I felt from the killer courses through me. "He hated her. Hated how greedy she was."

"Was?" Mitchell asks. "Are you saying she's dead?"

"I'm not sure. She knew him from the church. He said he needed her to sign a paper to move her uncle's body."

"Then he's not a church member," Mitchell says. "He works for the church."

I nod. "We need to talk to Pastor Evans and get a list of all the people working on moving the graves. The killer is on that list."

"One problem," Mitchell says. "It's late. There's no way Pastor Evans is at the church."

"Then look him up. Call the station and find a phone number or address. Do you remember if there was a house on the church property? He might live right there. We can go over and—"

Mitchell grabs me by my shoulders. "Slow down."

"I can't. We know how to find this guy now. We need to move."

"We'll go to the church and see if Pastor Evans lives on the property."

I nod, and we rush off in the direction of Mitchell's Explorer. I couldn't go home and rest now if I wanted to. This is it. I'm so close to finding this guy. I know it.

Mitchell puts the police light on top of the car, and we race back to the church. There's a house located on the very back of the property, but we spot the problem immediately. It's on the area affected by the sinkholes. There's no way anyone is currently living in the house. There's even caution tape across the front porch.

"He could be staying with relatives," I say. "Call the station and find out who he's related to in the area." I look all around, my hands on my hips as I try to control my

DRASTIC CRIMES CALL FOR DRASTIC INSIGHTS

erratic breathing. I can't come this close just to hit another roadblock. I just can't.

Mitchell has his phone to his ear, and I pull up a quick Google search, conducting my own research of the minister. I find several obituaries, leaving me to believe he has no remaining family in the area. I groan and pocket my phone.

"Nothing," Mitchell says. "He's the only—"

"Living relative in the area. Yeah, I know."

"Time to head home, Piper. He could be with any one of the members of the church. We can't go door to door searching for him."

I know he's right, and that only makes me angrier. This killer is beating me at every turn.

Mitchell brings me a cup of tea and sits on the other end of the couch so Jez can assume her usual position between us. Jez immediately puts her head in my lap, and I rest one hand on top of her to scratch behind her ear.

"This guy is almost all-knowing," Mitchell says. "He seems to be aware of everyone's routines. How is that the case when he works at the church? He might not even attend Sunday services. That's probably why you didn't sense him in the worship hall."

"In his mind, he's playing God. He's exacting his wrath on those he deems to be the worst sinners."

Mitchell sips his tea, and his brow furrows in thought. "Then what about him? Does he really believe his actions are justified?"

"I think he does." Something tugs at my insides. "There's more, though. He's so..." I ball my free hand, and

Jez's head jerks up, sensing my sudden mood swing. I'm channeling him again. "Angry. He's full of rage."

"Isn't anger another one of the seven deadly sins?" Mitchell places his teacup on the coffee table and turns so he's facing me with his back pressed up against the arm of the couch.

"It is." I sit up and place my teacup beside his. "So, let's recap." I hold up my hand and start ticking off on my fingers. "Maggie was targeted for her infidelity, which the killer defines as lust. Carmen was pride. Sky was envy. Monique was greed. What's left?"

Mitchell has his phone in hand. "We're missing sloth, gluttony, and anger."

At the mention of anger, the killer's rage fills me once more. "The killer is anger. This isn't just about punishing others. The killer knows he's sinning as well."

Mitchell scratches Jez, who has moved closer to him now that I'm sitting on the edge of the couch. "Why is his sin prevailing over the others', though?"

"Don't you see? He's the final victim. Anger. He's going to murder six people to stop them from ever sinning again, and then he plans to kill himself."

Mitchell's eyes widen. "So, this killing spree ends with suicide?"

"Unless we stop it before it gets to that point."

CHAPTER NINETEEN

The bell above the door announces my arrival at Marcia's Nook. Marcia is busy ringing up customers at the bakery counter, so I wander over to the mystery section in the back to browse the new titles even though Marcia said she had a book on hold for me. I almost run into a man reading the back cover of a book while roaming the aisles.

"I'm so sorry," I say, even though I'm pretty sure the near collision was more his fault than mine.

He looks up from the book and smiles. "Apologies are all mine. I'm afraid I get so wrapped up in what I'm reading I tend to forget the rest of the world exists. Does that ever happen to you?"

"All the time," I say.

He extends his hand. "I'm Adam by the way."

I hate shaking hands with strangers like this. For some reason, certain people are harder not to read than to read, and I never know who that will apply to before it's too late.

Adam lowers his hand to his side, and I realize I'm staring blankly at the space between us.

"Sorry," I say. "I'm somewhat of a germaphobe. It is flu

season and all." It's been my go-to excuse for years, but I still don't make it sound convincing.

He gives me an awkward nod and walks away without another word.

"That was painful to watch," Mitchell says, emerging from behind the next aisle.

"Yeah, well no one invited you to spy on me."

He holds up both hands. "I wasn't intentionally spying. I came here looking for you, and Marcia said you wandered back here."

I pretend to read the spines of the books on the shelf to my left. "Well, you found me. Any luck finding where Pastor Evans is staying?"

"Nope, but I figure we'll ask him as soon as you get your coffee and we head to the church."

"Great. Let's go then."

"No book?" Mitchell gestures to the shelf.

"Marcia has one at the register for me."

"Then what were you doing back here?" The corner of his mouth tips up ever so slightly. "Other than breaking that poor guy's heart, that is."

I glare at him. "What are you talking about? I don't even know that guy from—"

"Adam?" Mitchell laughs. "He was flirting with you, Piper. You must have picked up on that."

Flirting? No way. "All he did was try to shake my hand."

"Yeah, about that... Were you afraid you'd see his thoughts if you touched him?"

Yes. But they surely wouldn't have been about me.

"I can tell you what he was thinking, and I'm not even psychic."

"You think you know everything, don't you?"

"I know men, and I saw the way he was smiling at you. He thought he'd met an attractive woman who shared his love of reading, and he would have asked you out for coffee, if not dinner, if you'd only acknowledged his introduction in some way. But you wouldn't even give him your name."

"I don't have time to date. Haven't we been through this?"

"You hung out with me last night. You easily could have coffee with a guy."

"Not interested. End of story." Mitchell knows why I can't get close to people. I've already told him as much, so why is he pushing this issue? I walk past him to the register where Marcia has two coffees, my book, and a white pastry bag waiting for us. I take out my phone to pay, but Mitchell slaps a fifty on the countertop.

"I've got it."

"You're not paying for my book or my breakfast."

"It's both our breakfasts, and the book is insurance that I won't have to entertain you tonight, so it's my treat."

"Ha-ha." I quickly pay and motion to his money on the counter. "Don't forget that." I grab the bag and thank Marcia for the book.

"You two are always entertaining," Marcia says, leaning forward on the counter. "You should really come in more often. I miss you guys when you're too busy to stop in."

"Well, then we'll have to change that." Mitchell smiles as he picks up the fifty-dollar bill and places it in Marcia's tip jar.

"Detective, I can't accept that." Marcia immediately removes the bill and slides it across the counter, but Mitchell backs away.

"Sorry, but we're in a hurry. You'll have to hang on to that for me." He winks and gets the door for me.

Marcia looks completely stunned as we leave.

"Why do you do that?" I ask, mentally counting the twenty-three steps back to my office.

"Do what?"

"Don't play dumb with me. Why do you give her such insanely large tips?"

Mitchell pauses at my office door. "She has one employee helping her run that entire store. What does that tell you, Ms. Private Investigator?"

"She can't afford to hire anyone else."

"Exactly. She works hard, and she deserves those tips." He bobs one shoulder. "I have the extra cash, which I would be spending on dates if I actually dated anymore, so why not give it to someone who truly deserves the money? It's a no-brainer if you ask me." He opens the door before I can say more. Sometimes he really surprises me.

"Good morning," Dad says.

"What are you doing here so early?" I ask him, placing my coffee and bag on the desk. "I would have gotten you coffee if I'd known."

"I had some before I left the house this morning. I wanted to get here early to do a little research."

"What kind?" I sit down but don't put my purse in the bottom drawer since I don't plan to stay at the office for long. I need to talk to Pastor Evans and find out the names of everyone who is working in the cemetery right now.

"Well, when the case began, it seemed like the kidnapper was targeting women who rejected him."

"I hope for your sake it's not Adam," Mitchell says, winking at me.

"Who's Adam?" Dad asks.

"No one," I snap before taking a sip of my coffee. "Go on, Dad."

DRASTIC CRIMES CALL FOR DRASTIC INSIGHTS

"The whole forbidden fruit thing is tripping me up." He taps his index finger on the desk. "Why switch from forbidden fruit to the seven deadly sins?"

"Maybe he realized these women were the physical embodiments of the seven deadly sins, and that made him stray from his original plan."

Dad and I both stare at Mitchell.

"That was unusually insightful for you," I say, voicing what Dad and I are both thinking.

"Hey, I can have good insights, too. Just because you're the psychic doesn't mean you're the only one who can piece things together." He leans back in his chair.

"You're right, though. I can feel it. He started out targeting women who rejected him. But when he realized they had bigger faults, that they were all sinners in what he deems the worst ways, he switched tactics." I allow my mind to go completely blank, and I recall the killer's anger. "He's not just anger. He's all seven of the sins."

"What do you mean?" Mitchell sits forward and narrows his eyes at me. "Keep thinking out loud, Piper. I think you're onto something."

"He's lust because he lusts after women who rejected him. He's pride because he thinks the police will never catch him since he's keeping the bodies hidden and he's stopped leaving his calling card—the forbidden fruit. He's greed because he keeps taking more victims, and since it's never enough, he's also portraying gluttony. He envies his own genius in this plan he's concocted. Yet he's angry that he's sinning so much."

Mitchell counts on his fingers. "One is missing."

"Sloth," Dad says. "How is he displaying characteristics of sloth?"

"He will in his death. Instead of running or trying to

remain a free man after killing all these people, he'll kill himself. Death is the ultimate form of sloth in his mind. It's giving up." I swallow hard and shake my head, allowing myself to come out of my meditative state.

"Wow, Piper." Mitchell reaches across the desk, but I pull away because it's my right hand, and I don't want to accidentally read him now. My mind feels like mush after putting the killer's motives together like this. "Sorry," he says, leaning back in his seat again.

"It's okay. My mind is just very open at the moment, and I promised I wouldn't read you anymore."

He nods in understanding and then consults his watch. "If we leave now, we'll get to the church right around the time Pastor Evans usually does."

I stand up and grab the bag of food I neglected to even open. "Dad, you want to tag along?"

"No. I'm going to head to the morgue and find out if any bodies have turned up. I still can't figure out where the killer is hiding them all. That is if you're sure they're all dead."

I'm not sure they're *all* dead. Yet. But they will be. Soon. "Good thinking," I say.

Pastor Evans isn't exactly happy to see us. I can tell he was hoping we'd have this case cracked by now. He and I both. He gestures to the chairs across from his desk. "What can I do for you today?"

"We have reason to believe the kidnapper works for the church," Mitchell says, wording it much nicer than I would have.

Pastor Evans sits up straighter. "Works here?"

I can tell he thinks we're accusing him, so I add, "It's someone who is working on the grave relocation."

"Oh." He visibly relaxes. "I assume you'd like a list of all the employees on that project then so you can interview them."

Sure, why not let him think that's what our process will be. I nod.

He slides his chair a few inches to the left where his laptop is resting on the desk. No one says a word while he types away and then the printer behind him hums to life. He whirls around in his chair and pulls a paper off the printer tray. "Here you go." He holds the paper out to Mitchell but doesn't let go of it. "Detectives, I'd appreciate it if you could handle this with a little discretion. The church is under quite a bit of financial strain as it is with this relocation. If my members think it's not safe to attend services, I'm not sure how much longer any of us will be employed here."

"We understand," Mitchell says.

Pastor Evans finally releases the paper, and Mitchell passes it to me.

I take a deep breath and focus on the list of names. To my surprise, three pop out at me. I bring the paper closer to my face. "This can't be right."

"What is it?" Mitchell asks.

"I only sensed one killer."

"Killer? I thought this was a kidnapper you were looking for." Pastor Evans's tone is riddled with panic.

"Three names are popping out at me."

"Popping out? Detective, what is she talking about?"

I ignore the minister and direct my statement at Mitchell. "Lester Chapman, Randall Williams, and Pastor Evans."

Mitchell's head whips in the minister's direction. "Pastor, why would your name trigger Piper's radar?"

"What radar? What are you both talking about?" His tone is getting more panicked by the second, and his gaze volleys between Mitchell and me.

"Pastor, you're already aware of what I can do. When I look at a list of names, some jump out at me as being important. I don't always know why they're important, but your name is on this list."

"Yes, because I have to approve everything that concerns the church and its members."

"That's not why I'm seeing your name."

"You're seeing it because anyone who can read can see it." He gestures to the paper in my hand. "It's right there in black and white."

"Why are you getting so defensive?" Mitchell asks, sitting up straighter.

"This is my church. For you to accuse me of—"

"No one accused you of anything," I say. "Like I said, I don't always know why something is important when it presents itself to me." I lean forward and rest the paper on his desk. "You said my ability is a gift from God. Why does that suddenly seem to frighten you? You do want me to solve this case, don't you?"

"Of course I do, but I don't know why you'd be seeing my name in the way you're describing."

I don't know why either, but I highly doubt the good minister is going to allow me to read him right now. He's close to losing his mind. "We'll need to speak to Lester Chapman and Randall Williams."

"Lester took the day off, and Randall works on the night crew."

Mitchell and I exchange looks. Both conveniently

missing right after Monique was taken. He cocks his head, and I know he's wondering if Lester and Randall are working together. I shake my head. This is a solo operation. Which begs the question why are three names practically jumping off the page at me?

"Pastor, who are you staying with while your home is uninhabitable?"

He swallows so hard I see the lump in his throat. "I'm staying with Lester."

Well, things are starting to look a whole lot worse for the minister.

CHAPTER TWENTY

Mitchell looks ready to spring out of his chair and slap handcuffs on Pastor Evans, but I hold up my hand to stop him.

"Then I suppose you can take us to Lester's house right now so we can speak with him." I stand up, letting him know this isn't up for negotiation. "We really don't have any time to lose."

"Of course." Pastor Evan's voice squeaks, and he clears his throat as he stands. "Should I be worried I'm in danger?" he asks as he opens the office door for us.

"Depends on how well you know Lester," Mitchell says.

"He's not the best worker. He's often late and unkempt. But he did offer me a room when I needed one."

Because it required no effort on his part. *Sloth*. I grab Mitchell's arm as we walk out of the church to the parking lot. "Possible next victim," I whisper to him. Since I'm not sure how involved Pastor Evans is in all this, I can't let him know what I'm weaving together in my mind.

Mitchell looks in Pastor Evans's direction, but I give a

sharp shake of my head. "Sloth," I whisper, knowing he'll connect the word with Pastor Evans's description of Lester.

Knowing the next victim ahead of time could mean saving Lester and catching the killer. This is our first big break in the case.

Pastor Evans veers to the left. "My car is over here."

"I'll drive," Mitchell says. "I insist." It's clear he doesn't want to let the minister out of his sight.

"Very well," Pastor Evans says, falling in step with us again.

I spend the drive to Lester's house thinking about how convenient it is that Pastor Evans is living with the next victim. It does seem to implicate him as the killer, but how would he have kept that from me this entire time?

"It's that house there," Pastor Evans says, pointing to a ranch on the outskirts of town. The lawn is in dire need of cutting, and it doesn't look like anyone's cleaned the gutters in years. Yet Lester is part of the grounds crew at the church. That doesn't add up at all.

"Pastor, what made you hire Lester in the first place. I mean it's clear you're aware of his...shortcomings." I gesture to the property as we exit the vehicle.

"He has his faults, but he also has some redeeming qualities."

"Such as?" Mitchell's not convinced at all.

"Every church has its sinners. It's the minister's job to help the church's members become better people."

"And that's what you believe you're doing with Lester?" I ask, suddenly very interested in the minister's thinking, which seems to match the killer's thought process as well.

Mitchell must think so too because he pauses and places his hand on his hip, near where his gun is holstered under his jacket.

"I hope so. I believe it's what God wants me to do."

I'm pretty sure the killer believes that, too. Pastor Evans is doing nothing to clear his name in my mind. Still, I have no evidence against him. I start up the walkway, which is overgrown with weeds. Mitchell grabs me before I step over a crack in the cement filled with a tall patch of grass.

"What?" I ask.

"Snake. Don't move. It looks like a water moccasin."

I hate snakes. Despise them. My entire body goes rigid with fear, my leg still raised in the air.

Pastor Evans bends down slightly. "Yes. There's a stream that runs through the woods in the backyard. I've seen a few of these snakes in the yard, unfortunately. The warmer temperatures lately seem to have confused some of them and made them come back out. I'm afraid I'm not a fan of them."

"Neither am I." I look to Mitchell for some help.

He literally pulls me backward since I'm still paralyzed with fear. The snake spots us and slithers off into the overgrown garden in front of the house, and once it's out of sight, I shiver with disgust.

Pastor Evans studies me. "Interesting. Do you share my belief that snakes are the physical embodiment of the devil?"

"Like in the story of Adam in Eve?" Mitchell asks.

The minister nods. "Yes. It's states in the bible that because the snake tempted Eve, who in turn tempted Adam to eat from the tree of knowledge, man and snakes will always be enemies."

"See, Piper, your dislike of snakes is justified by the bible," Mitchell mocks me.

I don't care what the justification is. I just hate the vile creatures. They sneak up on you. "Can we go inside please?" I ask, moving toward the door.

Mitchell knocks even though Pastor Evans is technically living here at the moment. We wait for what seems like an impossibly long time, but when Lester doesn't answer, I turn to Pastor Evans, who consults his watch. "Lester usually sleeps until around eleven. He starts work right around that time." I don't miss his implication that Lester is typically late.

"He must be a sound sleeper," I say, considering Mitchell's knock was anything but quiet.

I try pressing the doorbell, but nothing happens. Apparently, Lester hasn't kept anything in working order around here.

"I assume you have a key," Mitchell says, stepping aside to let Pastor Evans by.

"Of course." The minister's hand shakes as he reaches into his pocket to retrieve the single key on a *Jesus Loves You* keychain. Why is he so nervous? Are we about to walk into the house to find Lester and the other missing people all dead in the basement or something? I'm not getting any bad vibes from the place, but I haven't exactly been tuning into my senses either. With the snake incident, I've been trying to tune out instead of in.

The door creaks as Pastor Evans pushes it open. The state of the entryway is appalling. The laminate flooring has holes in it. I'm not even sure how that happens. And the walls are a muted beige color coated in so much dust I'm convinced this place has never been cleaned.

"Please excuse the appearance. I've only had time to clean the room above the garage. That's where I've been staying." Pastor Evans walks inside and calls out to Lester. "Lester, are you awake yet?"

It's still well before Lester's wake-up time according to Pastor Evans, so I'm assuming we'll find him asleep in his room.

Pastor Evans turns to the left at the top of the stairs. We pass a bathroom on the right, and then Pastor Evans knocks on the next door, which is closed. When Lester doesn't answer, Pastor Evans turns the doorknob. "Lester?"

The room is completely dark, so I flip on a light switch on the wall by the door. The second I do, I regret the decision. The bed is unmade with an empty pizza box resting on one pillow. There's a pile of dirty clothes at the foot of the bed, and the dresser drawers are all pulled open with clothing spewing out of them. It looks like the room was ransacked, but my senses are telling me this is its usual state.

The brown carpeting is full of lint and other debris I don't even want to attempt to identify. Mitchell steps into the room, and his shoes kick up dust. "He's clearly not here."

I step out of the room, fanning my face to rid my nostrils of the smell of rotten food and garbage. "Where else would he be?"

"I don't know," Pastor Evans says, closing the door again once we're all in the hallway. "This is highly unusual. Lester never gets up a moment earlier than he needs to."

Mitchell's gaze falls on me, and I know what he's thinking. With no clue where Lester is, I'm going to have to read something in this place. I'm not stepping foot inside that room again, though. I make my way down the hall to the living room. The couch cushions are nearly concave, indicating Lester spends an awful lot of time on the piece of furniture, which makes it a good object to read.

I walk over and sit down on the couch, instantly sinking into the cushions.

Mitchell stifles a laugh. "You look lost in there. Do you need a hand getting out?"

"Ha-ha." I have sunk down into the frame, though. How is this comfortable for Lester? Instead of fighting against the piece of furniture trying to swallow me whole, I lie back, getting fully into the body indent.

"I'll call in the jaws of life to get you out when you're ready."

"Pastor, please excuse Detective Brennan's inappropriate jokes at a time when he should be concentrating on solving this case."

"Ms. Ashwell, what exactly are you doing?" Pastor Evans asks, standing over me.

"I'm going to read the energy off this couch to see if I can locate Lester." I close my eyes when Pastor Evans's mouth falls open. I don't have time for his cynicism or judgmental stares. He starts to say something, but Mitchell must stop him because he cuts himself off abruptly.

I focus on the couch. On finding Lester where he is now.

Darkness.

Silence.

At rest.

No. That can't be it. Of all the times for my senses to only give me whispers of a vision... I squeeze my hands into fists at my sides.

"Piper? Are you okay?" Mitchell asks, and I can feel his presence very near my body. Hovering.

I need to see more. *Show me more!*

Nothing comes.

I raise my right hand and slam it down on the cushion beside me. The couch creaks and groans, and the next thing

I know, Mitchell's arms are wrapped around me. I open my eyes to see the couch has collapsed in the middle.

"Thanks," I say, grateful for once that he was being overprotective during one of my visions—or in this case lack of vision since all I saw was darkness.

"Did it work? Did you see anything? You seemed stressed."

I push gently against Mitchell's chest, and he puts me on my feet before releasing his grip. I let out a deep breath. "All I saw was darkness. I think Lester might be asleep wherever he is."

"That doesn't surprise me," Pastor Evans says. "I've had other employees tell me Lester falls asleep on the job a lot. There are benches in the cemetery, and he tends to sleep on those."

"But would he really be at work this early?" Mitchell asks. "It doesn't seem to fit his MO."

No, it doesn't. "Did he possibly have a date last night?" I ask. "Could he have slept over at someone else's house?"

"I suppose it's possible." Pastor Evans doesn't seem happy with this explanation, most likely because it would mean Lester was engaging in activities that defy Pastor Evans's beliefs. I can't imagine he'd look lightly on something like premarital sex.

"It was only a guess. I couldn't tell where he was. I just know he's asleep."

My phone rings in my purse, which is on the floor beside the couch. I must have dropped it when I sank back into the cushion. I snatch it up and grab my phone, seeing Dad's name on the screen.

"Hey, Dad. What did you find out?"

"We have a Jane Doe at the morgue. A burn victim. This could be any one of the three missing women." He pauses. "I'm sorry to ask you to do this, pumpkin, but I don't think we have any other choice. I need you to read the remains so we can ID the body."

I swallow back the bile working its way up my throat. IDing a burn victim is enough to make anyone lose their breakfast. But reading one is... I'm most likely going to be out of commission for the rest of the day after the vision this will give me. I just hope the woman wasn't burned alive.

CHAPTER TWENTY-ONE

Mitchell stops at Matty's Subs on the way to the morgue for two reasons: I need to refuel before this vision, and I might not be able to eat for a week after what I'm about to do.

I finish my turkey and American cheese on rye bread just as we pull up to the back entrance of the hospital where the morgue is located. I crumble the paper the sandwich was wrapped in and open the door.

Mitchell meets me on my side of the car. "Hey." His tone is soft, and his hand rests lightly on my left forearm. "Is there anything I can do to make this a little easier on you?"

I consider it for a moment. "Yeah. Whatever you do, don't let them put me in a room and hook me up to an IV. Just get me home." I can't afford to be stuck in a hospital under observation for fake symptoms brought on by a horrific vision.

He nods. "You got it." His hand raises and squeezes the side of my arm.

"Don't pity me, Mitchell."

"I'm not. I'm in awe of your bravery at the moment."

"Is that a rare Mitchell Brennan compliment?" I cock my head at him.

He blinks several times and shakes his head like he's trying to rid himself of a thought. "Sorry. Don't know what came over me. I won't let it happen again."

"Good." I walk past him and open the door to the morgue.

Mitchell flashes his badge at the woman we nearly run into. "Detective Mitchell Brennan. My partner and I got a call to come ID a body."

"They're with me," Dad calls from behind the woman.

She turns and nods to Dad before walking outside. She must be on her break, which bodes well for me. I don't need any witnesses.

Dad walks over and hugs me. As much as I try to shield myself from it, I can feel the fear pouring off him. His embrace is meant to comfort me, yet it's doing anything but. It's times like this that I see my abilities as a curse. To not be able to hug your own father without cringing isn't fair. He releases me, and I breathe deeply to rid myself of his emotions.

Mitchell is studying me, and somehow I know he's picked up on what just happened. I give him a small smile to let him know I'm okay.

"Where's the body?" I ask, wanting to get this over with.

Dad motions to a door leading to another room. "In there. I have to warn you it isn't pretty. There are no recognizable features. I'm hoping you can get a quick vision to tell us who she is and how this happened. Then get out."

Mitchell eyes me. "Can you do that? Willingly leave a vision?"

"It's not easy, but I can." As long as I'm not overwhelmed by the death. "I might need a little help, though."

Mitchell rests his hand on the small of my back. "The second I see you're in pain, I'll sever your connection to the body."

Dad's gaze volleys between us. I know what he's thinking. I have to stop pushing Mitchell away. He understands me, or he's at least trying to. And maybe I do need another friend besides Marcia.

"Don't do it too soon. I need to see as much as I can because I'm not going to be able to bring myself to do this more than once."

They both stare at me, waiting for me to say I'm ready and not wanting to rush me. The problem is I'll never be ready to experience someone dying. It never gets easier. I inhale a few deep breaths and give a slight nod before starting for the room with the body.

The smell of charred flesh hits me as soon as I open the door. Dad holds out two masks and already has one on his face. Mitchell puts his on, but I decline mine. I need to tune into all my senses, no matter how horrifying that may be. The form on the table is indescribable. I can barely stomach the sight and smell of it, and yet I have to somehow bring myself to touch it.

Mitchell matches my every step, and I can feel his gaze on me. I do my best to tune him out while also allowing myself the comfort of knowing he's here to bring me out of the vision when it gets to be too much. As unpleasant as it is to breathe deeply in the presence of the body, I have to clear my mind and I don't know any other way to do it. I take a few calming breaths and close my eyes. Then I raise my right hand and place it on top of the arm closest to me.

A boat cabin comes into view. The rocking sensation of the waves causes the boat to bob up and down. The woman is sitting on a small bed, brushing her long red hair. The door to the cabin opens, and a tall man with dark hair and dark eyes walks in.

"I thought you were making us breakfast," he says, anger in his tone.

"I will once I finish getting ready."

"If I wanted such insolence, I would have asked my wife to come with me on this trip."

The woman stands up, tossing her brush on the bed behind her. "You throw her in my face every chance you get."

"At least she can cook. You're only good for one thing, Greta."

She grabs the brush and throws it at his head, but he quickly ducks behind the door, slamming it shut. She breaks down and sobs on the bed for a moment. "I don't know why I even bother with you." She wipes her eyes and stands up before going to the hot plate on the small dresser. "You want breakfast? I'll make you your damn breakfast."

She turns on the small burner before picking up her brush. She resumes brushing her hair, counting the strokes and calming herself in the process. Once she's finished, she hugs one of the pillows on the bed and closes her eyes.

She wakes up to the smell of smoke. Her eyes widen at the sight of the flames coming from the hot plate. The entire dresser is on fire, and it's spreading quickly throughout the small cabin. She rushes to the door, but the flames block her path.

"Everett!" she screams. "Everett, help!" She chokes on the smoke. "Damn it, Everett! Help me!"

She falls to her knees, wheezing.

My hand is pulled from the body, and Mitchell is gripping my arms, holding me upright as I fight to get air in my lungs.

"Piper, look at me. Focus on me. It wasn't real. You can fight this. We're in the morgue. You're safe."

I peer into his green eyes, and my breathing calms. He doesn't release me until I'm breathing normally again.

"Impressive," Dad says. "I've never seen her recover so quickly." He walks over to me and looks me up and down. "How do you feel?"

"Okay." My voice is raspy, but I'm much better than I thought I'd be. "Mitchell stopped the vision before Greta burned to death."

"Greta?" Dad asks.

"Yeah. She was on a boat with the man she was having an affair with. They argued about his wife being a better cook. Greta was going to try to prove him wrong, but she fell asleep with the hot plate on. Everything went up in flames, and she was trapped in the room. She called out to the man. Everett was his name. But he wasn't there."

Mitchell lowers his mask, whips out his phone, and turns away from us. "This is Brennan. Did anyone pick up a man named Everett? He was most likely sailing the Delaware on a small boat with a cabin. The woman with him died on the boat, burned to death." He pauses. "Uh-huh. Yeah, call him back in. He didn't cause the fire, but he knew the victim, though I'm sure he'll try to deny it since he was having an affair with her." Another pause. "How do you think I know?" His tone isn't the least bit friendly, and it's clear whoever he's talking to at the station isn't a fan of mine. "Just do it. We need him to ID the body in the morgue." He hangs up and turns back to us. "Everett Gilbert was pulled out of the Delaware River yesterday afternoon. He'd been swimming and said he lost track of where he was and couldn't find his way back to the boat."

"Sounds suspicious," Dad says.

"He claims he was pulled downstream by the current."

"More like he was out swimming when the fire started, and when he saw his boat go up in flames, he swam as far away from it as he could because staying would mean implicating him for having an affair."

Dad and Mitchell both stare at me.

"Fact," I say, knowing they're questioning how I came upon this information. "That's what happened."

"I'll let Wallace know." Mitchell gets on his phone again.

Officer Wallace is one of the few down at the Weltunkin PD who believes in what I can do. I wish Mitchell called him in the first place, but it is what it is.

"We need to get looking for Lester Chapman," I say, leaving the room and heading for the parking lot. I take huge gulps of fresh air as Dad and I wait for Mitchell to finish his call.

"How bad was it?" Dad asks.

"Nowhere near as bad as I thought it would be—thanks to Mitchell." It's hard to admit how helpful Mitchell's been to me. Even more so to say it out loud.

"I'm glad you two are getting along again. He's trying really hard to be there for you, and I think he's doing a damn good job of it."

I lean against the passenger door. "I know. I'm trying too, Dad. I really am."

"But it's harder for you. I get that, pumpkin. I just don't want to see you spend your life alone."

"I have my work, and you and Mom, and Jez, and Marcia—"

"And Mitchell," he adds before I can chance leaving him off the list.

"See. I'm not alone at all."

The back door opens, and Mitchell walks out. "I've got news."

I stand up straight. "About Everett or the case?"

"The case. I had Wallace run a name for me while we were on the phone." He doesn't need to tell me which name, but he does anyway. "There's no Randall Williams listed in Weltunkin."

"So it's a fake name."

"Looks like it."

And it looks like we have a positive ID on the killer.

CHAPTER TWENTY-TWO

Dad jerks his thumb over his shoulder. "I'm going to head back to the office and see what I can dig up on this Randall Williams guy."

I nod. "Mitchell and I will head to the church and see what we can find out there." Randall works the night shift, and we'll stay at the church until then if necessary.

"Good luck. And stay in touch if you find anything." Dad gives a wave as he heads to his BMW.

"Same goes for you." I open the car door and get in.

Mitchell's phone rings, and his brow furrows at the unfamiliar number on the screen. I nod for him to answer it. With four open cases, the call could be about any one of the women we're searching for. Any one of their bodies could have been discovered.

Mitchell answers the phone on speaker so I can hear. "Detective Brennan."

"Detective, this is Pastor Evans."

Mitchell and I share a look.

"What can I do for you, Pastor?"

"Lester didn't show up for work today. No one has seen him."

His voice is riddled with emotions, pain being the most dominant. His church is his family. He cares about every one of these people, and the loss of so many of them is taking a definite toll on him.

"We're on our way there now, Pastor," Mitchell says.

"Thank you, Detective. I appreciate you giving my church and its members your immediate attention like this."

He may not be so happy about the attention the church is going to get soon. It's clear the only way we're going to solve this case is if I publicly reveal what I can do and read just about everyone and everything in that place. I can't imagine this ending well.

Mitchell disconnects the call and puts the light back on top of his Explorer.

The entire ride to the church, my vision of Lester plays in my mind. It takes me a while, but by the time we reach the church parking lot, I'm gripping my seat belt. "Oh my God!"

"Not the place to use the Lord's name in vain, Piper," Mitchell says as he parks the car.

"My vision. I was wrong. Lester wasn't asleep."

"Is he dead?"

I unclick my seat belt. "No. He was unconscious."

"So the kidnapper knocked him out."

"Just like he knocked out Carmen in the park."

"Are you sensing chloroform? Did you smell it in your vision of Lester?"

I shake my head. "No, but he was already unconscious, so I wouldn't have smelled it."

Mitchell drums his fingers on the steering wheel. "Time to play a little game?"

DRASTIC CRIMES CALL FOR DRASTIC INSIGHTS

I didn't think I'd be up to using my abilities at all for the rest of the day, but thanks to Mitchell, I feel fine. I nod but hold one finger up in the air as I clear my mind. I lean my head back against the headrest, and once I'm ready, I lower my finger.

"What's your least favorite animal?"

"Snake."

"What book are you reading?"

"*Murder, Murder Everywhere.*"

"What day is it?"

"Thursday."

"Why is the kidnapper using chloroform on the victims?"

"Because he needs to bury them before they wake up."

"Where is he burying them?"

I can't answer Mitchell's question because my last response has me so shaken up it jostles me out of my meditative state. I turn my head to look at him, not sure how he was able to keep up his line of questioning after I dropped that crucial piece of information. "The killer is burying his victims. That's why no one has discovered any of the bodies."

"But where is he burying them?"

"It could be anywhere. His backyard." That wouldn't be a first for a case I've worked on.

"Are you saying that because you think its right?"

"No. I'm guessing now." I tap the side of my head. "Things are cloudy up here again."

Mitchell finally undoes his seat belt. "Let's get inside and talk to Pastor Evans. Maybe he can help us find Lester and Randall."

We pass a group of kids as we head inside. It looks like there's a church preschool class going on and it's recess or something. Luckily for them, the playground area isn't near the cemetery.

The door to Pastor Evans's office is open, which is unusual. Mitchell knocks on the open door anyway.

Pastor Evans looks up at us and rubs the front of his face with one palm. "Please come in."

We step inside and sit down.

"Pastor, I believe Lester is already in danger. The kidnapper is using chloroform to knock out his victims and..." How do I say this to a clearly distraught minister?

"He's burying them," Mitchell finishes for me.

Pastor Evans narrows his eyes. "You mean he's kidnapping people, killing them, and then burying the bodies?"

"No." I swallow hard. "He's burying them alive."

Pastor Evans's face pales to the point where he looks like a corpse. "A-alive? So they're..."

"Pastor, time is of the utmost importance right now. We need to find Lester." We don't know when Randall buried him, so we don't know if he's run out of air yet.

"But you don't know where they're being buried, do you?"

Yes! I do. How didn't I see this sooner? "Lester worked with Randall," I blurt out.

"They never actually worked the same shift, but they both worked in the..." Pastor Evans meets my gaze. "Dear Lord. Are you saying my church members are being buried alive"—his index finger jabs the top of his desk—"in *this* cemetery?"

And by one of Pastor Evans's employees. If the church doesn't close after all this, I'll be shocked. "Pastor, do we have your permission to dig in the cemetery?"

He nods. "Yes. Please, go find them. Hurry. I'll alert my

crew to cease work immediately. But I must warn you the area with the sinkholes is extremely unstable."

Mitchell and I stand up. "Thank you," I say. I want to tell him we'll find Lester in time. That no one else will die on church property, but I can't. The death count isn't over yet. I can feel it.

The minister picks up his phone as we exit the office. I'm sure he's calling his workers to let them know we'll be needing access to the cemetery and their equipment.

"Any chance you know how to use one of those machines?" I ask Mitchell as we step outside and the bucket loader comes into view.

"Can't be that difficult, right? I mean, the graves must be freshly dug."

"That's true, but is Randall burying his victims in the old section with the sinkholes or in the new section? New graves would seem too obvious."

"Thinking aloud again? Or are you onto something?" Mitchell stops short of the cemetery entrance.

"Not sure yet. What do you think?"

He looks out at the headstones. Several are overturned from the unsteady ground. "Old section. No one would notice it among this mess. He might even be hoping that the sinkholes swallow the bodies."

A man in a reflective vest and hardhat walks over to us. "You must be the detectives Pastor Evans called me about." He extends his gloved hand. "I'm Milton. I'm overseeing the project during the day shift."

Working the day shift probably means he doesn't know Randall.

Mitchell introduces us.

"I've told my crew to take the rest of the day off, so the

place is all yours. Do you want me to stay and help out with the machinery, or have you operated one of these before?" He motions to the bucket loader.

Most of what I'm going to do involves sensing the victims. But having Milton around to do the actual digging isn't a bad idea.

"Is it safe to drive that thing with the ground being compromised?" Mitchell asks.

"Depends where the grave is that we're digging up. We have to do a lot by hand." He motions to a pile of shovels near the cemetery gate.

Metal is one of the best objects for me to read because it tends to radiate energy. If Randall used one of those shovels, I might be able to tell where he dug the graves. "I think we can handle the digging. We'll do it by hand."

Mitchell cocks his head at me, and I slap my left hand down on his shoulder. "This one loves manual labor." I smile at Milton, wanting him gone so I can read the shovels without an audience.

"Suit yourself. I'll stick around inside with Pastor Evans in case you two change your mind and want some help."

"Thank you. We appreciate that," I say as he walks back toward the church.

"What are you thinking?" Mitchell asks.

I start for the shovels. "Randall must have used one of these, right?"

"True. But how well can you read the shovel if Randall wore gloves?"

"I can still do it." I stop right before the pile of shovels. There are about eight of them. The odds that Randall used the same shovel each time are slim, so it's possible he's touched several of these. I reach for the first one and hold it in both hands. Closing my eyes, I allow the energy in the metal to flow to me.

Lester leans against the handle of the shovel, the bottom portion sunk into the ground.

Milton looks up from where he's shoveling. "You can't take another break, Lester. You just had one twenty minutes ago."

"I'm exhausted. This is hard work."

"Be happy it isn't the middle of the summer. Or the dead of winter. The ground hasn't had time to freeze yet."

I drop the shovel, not needing to see more since the vision is about Lester and not Randall. "This would be easier if it were nighttime," I say.

"Finding graves in the dark doesn't seem easier." Mitchell puts the shovel I discarded to the side. "Not to mention it's much colder at night."

"But the night crew worked with Randall. They'd be more helpful than Milton."

"What I don't understand is how Randall knows so much about all these church workers and members when he works the night shift. When does he even see them?"

"Call Pastor Evans. Find out if Randall is involved with the church in any other way. Also find out how long he's been employed here."

"So find out anything and everything I can." He nods and removes his phone from inside his jacket.

I pick up the next shovel. Before I even start reading it, the anger radiating from the metal assaults my senses. The rage is so familiar I know Randall used this shovel. I close my eyes and brace myself for what I'll see.

Damn sinners. All of you. You come here every Sunday, thinking that gives you a free pass. But He sees all. He knows what you do the other six days of the week. I know. I know none of you is worthy of this life. You belong in the ground, bugs feasting on your flesh.

"Piper!" Mitchell yells, ripping the shovel from my hand.

I'm about to yell at him for yanking me out of the vision but stop when I see the horrified look on his face. "What did I do?" I look around, trying to find any indication of what I did to freak him out so much.

"You swung this thing at my head."

That's why he grabbed it. "Oh my God." I press my hand to my mouth. "Mitchell, I'm so sorry. I didn't know I was doing it."

"I know." He tosses the shovel aside.

"What are you doing? I have to read that again." I start for it, but he grabs my arm.

"You're not touching that shovel. His rage is consuming you."

I've seen and felt murderers in visions before, but this guy... He's completely unhinged. I can't let him control me. I almost hit Mitchell. What if he hadn't been paying that close attention to me in the vision and the shovel actually connected with his head?

"Piper, breathe." Mitchell looks deep into my eyes, his hands cupping both sides of my face. "I'm okay. You didn't hurt me."

I don't know how he knows what I'm so upset about. I've never had anyone know me as well as he does. It's a little unnerving but also comforting at the same time.

"I have to find these people without injuring anyone in the process."

Mitchell lets go of me and picks up the shovel he tossed

aside. He stares at it before meeting my gaze again. "Can you use this to locate the victims without having another vision?"

"You mean use it like a metal detector except I'd be sensing similar energy instead?" That just might be crazy enough to work. I hold out my left hand. "I can try."

When he sees which hand it is, he willingly relinquishes the shovel. "Is there any way I can ground you here so you don't slip into a vision?"

I've never tried anything like that before, so I'm not sure it's possible. "I don't know. My plan is to sort of keep the shovel in my left hand and just hover my right hand near it so I can get a good read on the energy. Then we walk around until I feel the same energy coming from somewhere else."

Mitchell narrows his eyes in thought. "What if...?" He walks to my right side, his gaze trained on the hand I need to read objects. "Sorry," he says, "I know you're going to hate this, but it's all I can think of." He laces his fingers through mine.

I can't remember the last time someone held my hand, and I resist the burning sensation of tears behind my eyes. This isn't the time to sulk about my lack of human contact thanks to this ability.

"Try not to read me, okay?" he says, bumping his shoulder into mine.

"Why? Are you having inappropriate thoughts again?"

"When am I not?" he jokes.

I smile, and he takes a step in the direction of the first grave. "Thanks," I say. "For trying to help me through this."

"We're partners. It's what we do."

"I'm sorry I keep pushing you away every time we seem

to be making progress as friends. I'm sort of conditioned to do that."

"I assumed as much." He gently squeezes my hand. "I'm not going anywhere, Piper. You may not see it, despite your abilities, but you're helping me just as much as I'm helping you. I think I understand why my mom allowed herself to get on the plane that day. I think she thought she had to die or something bad might happen to my brother and me."

"I think so, too. I got the sense your mother was afraid of her abilities and even more afraid of defying them. I'm sorry."

He stops walking. "I spent years thinking my mom chose to die rather than raise my brother and me. For the first time, I see she chose to die because she thought it was the only way she could protect us. I never would have come to that understanding and the peace it gives me if not for you."

"Damn. When did we get so sappy?"

"You don't always have to resort to jokes, Piper."

Yes, I do because I don't like the way he's looking at me or the emotions I'm sensing from him despite trying not to read him. He's confusing his gratitude for feelings for me, and I can't let that happen.

"You know that's who I am. I can't change, Mitchell. Just like I can't help having these abilities or getting myself involved in cases like this. Speaking of..." I gesture to some overturned headstones off to our left. "I think we need to head in that direction." I don't actually sense anything. I just need him to focus on the case again.

Mitchell doesn't say another word. He might not be psychic, but he's clearly picked up on how uncomfortable he was making me.

We walk around as carefully as possible, trying to avoid sinkholes, which makes sensing energy nearly impossible. I'm not sure how the workers are moving these graves without tumbling into them. As if the ground can hear my thoughts, my foot sinks beneath the dirt and the earth swallows me.

CHAPTER TWENTY-THREE

"I've got you!" Mitchell yells. He's on the ground, lying down so he doesn't lose his grip on me.

My feet feel the solid ground beneath me. "I'm okay. I have some footing."

"I don't trust that footing. The ground just let loose under you. It could do it again."

"No, it can't," I say. "Not completely at least. I'm standing in a grave."

"I still don't trust it. Let me pull you up."

"No. Not yet. I have an idea."

"Piper, this is too dangerous. Just drop the shovel and give me your other hand so I can pull you out."

Not happening. At least the pulling me out part. "I have to read the grave to see if Randall touched this one. Let go."

"Are you insane? I'm not letting go of you!" His grip tightens.

"You're going to have to. You're holding my right hand." I try to pull it from him, but he's not relenting. "Mitchell, you are not my father, and even if you were, I'm a grown woman. You don't get to tell me what I can and can't do.

DRASTIC CRIMES CALL FOR DRASTIC INSIGHTS

Now let go." I give a final tug of my hand, and he releases me. My feet are steady on the top of the casket. "See. I'm fine."

Mitchell doesn't move from his position, ready to grab me again if necessary. "Just hurry up and do this so I can get you out of there."

I bend down and place my right hand on top of the casket.

A little girl no older than five places a rose on top of the casket and then skips back to her mother, who is crying onto a man's shoulder. She bends down and hugs the girl, who clearly doesn't understand the concept of a funeral.

I stand back up. "Nothing." I look at the shovel in my left hand.

"Give me your hand," Mitchell says.

It's dark, and this could be my last shot to find something helpful tonight.

"Piper, don't even think about it. We can take the shovel if you want. We'll bring it back to your place. It's safer to have a vision there anyway."

But that would mean abandoning Lester. Leaving him for dead.

"Ask me questions." My voice shakes. "I need to know if I can save Lester tonight."

Mitchell huffs, but he obliges. "What's your favorite flavor of coffee?"

"Toasted almond," I say.

"What did we find in Maggie's lunch bag?"

"An apple."

"When was the last time you attended a church service?"

"When I was eleven."

"What's your dog's name?"

"Jezebel."

"Is Lester Chapman alive?"

"No." Damn it. I stand up and reach for Mitchell, but he takes the shovel first so he can use both hands to pull me out of the sinkhole. "I'm sorry," he says once we're on our way back to the church.

"I'm starting to realize I'm going to lose more people than I save."

"It's the unfortunate truth of what we do." Mitchell tries the doors on the church, but they're locked. "I guess we missed Pastor Evans."

We were searching for a while. "Let's go. I'll try to read this shovel at home, and we'll hopefully find Randall Williams tomorrow."

Mitchell drives us back to my place and immediately walks Jezebel for me. I wonder what Jez thinks of Mitchell and me. He's always here, always taking her for walks. God, we have this totally dysfunctional relationship I couldn't define if I wanted to. And I definitely don't want to.

I lie down on the couch, clutching the shovel against my chest, and stare up at the ceiling. At some point, I drift off to sleep.

"You're the worst one of all, Pastor. You harp about all our sins, but what about yours? You're never satisfied. Never happy with what you have or what we give you. You're gluttonous. One of the worst sinners, and you don't even see it."

"Randall, please," Pastor Evans says from his bound position on the floor of the dark room.

"Come on now, Pastor. You of all people can't possibly be

DRASTIC CRIMES CALL FOR DRASTIC INSIGHTS

afraid to die. Where is your faith?" Randall leans down and grabs Pastor Evans's face. "Or are you afraid your sins will keep you from spending your afterlife in Heaven? Is that it, Pastor?"

Pastor Evans is visibly shaking now. "What do you want from me, Randall?"

"I want you to pay for your sins. I want you to beg for forgiveness."

"Fine. I beg your forgiveness, Randall. Please, give me a chance to make this right." The minister presses his palms together. Possibly praying or pleading. Maybe both.

"Ah, you are asking the wrong person. Though I see your confusion. My sin lies in my judgment and anger toward all of you. I will be judged for that. Just as you will be judged for your sins. We will both pay, Pastor. I promise you that." He yanks Pastor Evans to his feet. "It's time."

"Time for what? What are you going to do?"

"Give you a proper burial as you exit this life and face your final judgment."

"No. Randall, please."

"Don't worry. I've chosen a very special resting place for you. I think you'll be pleased." Randall pulls Pastor Evans from the utility shed on the church property and over to an open grave. The casket beside it isn't empty. A skeleton deteriorated by time rests inside.

Pastor Evans screams.

I bolt straight up on the couch, letting the shovel fall from my hand to the floor. Jezebel barks, and I open my eyes to realize I'm screaming. I quiet, and she nuzzles her head under my chin.

Mitchell is squatting next to me.

"You stayed?" I ask.

"I was afraid something like this would happen." He

moves the shovel farther away from the couch as if he's worried I'll try reading it again. I'm not going to do that.

"Pastor Evans is the final victim before Randall takes his own life."

Mitchell's eyes widen.

"I saw Randall with him. He buried him in the church cemetery. On the new side. He's using..." I pause to gulp in air since I haven't taken a single breath since the vision ended. "He's putting his victims in the caskets that are being dug up and reburied in the new section."

"Oh my God." He stands up and drags a hand through his hair. "Did you see where he buried Pastor Evans?"

"No. I only saw the open casket with the body. I don't know where he buried it." The work in the cemetery has ceased thanks to the investigation, which means Randall has the entire place to himself. We gave him the perfect opportunity to finish his plan. The thought makes me sick to my stomach. "We need to go right now. We can still save Pastor Evans."

Mitchell grabs his keys off the coffee table, and we're out the door with our jackets on in under sixty seconds. According to my phone, it's 4:32 a.m. Too early to call Dad. Mitchell must not want to bother him at this time of the morning either because he calls the station for backup instead. I look up how long a person can survive buried alive. To my dismay, there are YouTube videos on this very thing. No wonder killers these days have no trouble committing crimes. Stupid people leave video instructions on how to pull them off. My fist clenches in fury as I discover we have about five and a half hours from the time Pastor Evans was sealed inside the casket. The problem is I don't know when that was.

With the police light flashing on top of Mitchell's car

DRASTIC CRIMES CALL FOR DRASTIC INSIGHTS

and the fact that there aren't many cars on the roads at this time of night, we make it to the cemetery in record time. Mitchell drives right to the new section, and we jump out the second he cuts the engine.

"Look for a fresh grave," I say. "Possibly an open grave, too. I don't know if Randall put himself in a casket yet or is waiting until tomorrow." So far, he's only taken one person a night, but he must have realized work was ceased at the cemetery for a reason. He hasn't shown up for work or talked to anyone but his victims in at least a day, so that could mean he knows we're on to him. And that could have caused him to expedite the remainder of his plan.

We run through the cemetery to a freshly dug grave. Mitchell has the shovel we brought back to my place, and he immediately starts digging. That's going to take more time than we have though, especially since there are too many new graves to begin with. We need the bucket loader.

I run over to it, but the key isn't in the ignition. I race over to the utility shed since that's where Randall had Pastor Evans. The key must be there. I pull the door open and search for a light switch. Once the room is illuminated, I spot a set of keys hanging from a hook on the wall. I feel the energy radiating from them before I even make contact. Randall's rage is all over them. One in particular. I grab the key and hurry back to the bucket loader.

"What are you doing?" Mitchell calls to me.

"Speeding this up." I allow myself to focus on the energy of the key. Images of Randall operating the bucket loader fill my mind. I mimic his actions as I insert the key and turn it to the right. I press the throttle forward a little, depress the brakes and clutch, and then press the ignition button above the key. The engine starts, and I push the throttle all the way forward.

"Do you know what you're doing?" Mitchell yells.

"No, but Randall does. Now be quiet." I have to fully immerse myself in the vision to operate this machine. I allow the images in my mind to take over, and I drive the machine to the grave Mitchell is digging. He backs out of my way.

I scoop the dirt, which thankfully is soft thanks to the warmer weather we've been having. Once I hit the casket, I back up the machine to give us room and hop out to help Mitchell by hand from here. We have to use the shovel to dig around the edges of the casket so we can get it open. It takes both of us to pry off the lid. Luckily it's not sealed tightly. Randall was using the weight of the dirt—six feet of it—to keep the caskets closed. I'm also convinced Pastor Evans was the only one who was buried while still conscious. Randall wanted him to suffer the most.

Mitchell opens the lid to see a woman I know is Maggie Burns. I turn away, not wanting this image of her to be burned in my brain forever. And that's when I notice another grave, freshly dug and not recovered with dirt. "There! Randall couldn't fully bury himself. That has to be him!"

Mitchell lowers the lid on Maggie's casket and rushes over to the open grave with me. Mitchell tries to open the lid of the casket, but it won't budge.

"He must have sealed himself in there somehow." He wants to die, to punish himself for his sins, and clearly, he designed this casket to lock from the inside and be airtight.

Mitchell uses the shovel like a crowbar, which winds up breaking the wooden lid. We pry the lid of the casket up to see Randall's face twisted in rage. He's slow to move, which means he's been buried for a while and the carbon dioxide he's been breathing has slowed his body function significantly.

Mitchell immediately cuffs him before he can attempt to get away, not that I think he'd have any chance of doing that in his current state. He can't even speak coherently. His words are nothing but mutters. And that means he can't tell us where Pastor Evans is buried, not that I think he would.

"Piper, can you read him?" Mitchell asks me.

"Get him out of the grave. He needs medical attention."

"What are you going to do? We have to find Pastor Evans."

"We're going to. Just get him out of the casket." I can't get on with my plan until Randall is moved since he's currently occupying the space I need to read.

Mitchell hoists Randall out of the ground and reads him his rights before calling the station for backup.

I lower myself into the casket, which is creepy enough as it is, but considering it's also occupied by a skeleton, this is downright horrifying. Still, I'm not touching Randall. Even handcuffed, I know he'd try to kill me somehow if I came into contact with him. I'd never get a good read with him struggling against me, and time is of the essence.

I close my eyes and pretend there isn't a human skull next to my head.

"What's wrong, Pastor. I thought you'd be happy to be buried with your very own grandfather. It's really a lot more than you deserve, don't you think? I mean, you were named after him. Or do you think he'll be upset you chose not to marry and have a son to become Chandler Evans the Fourth?"

That's all I need to see. "He's buried in Chandler Evans's grave." I climb out of the casket, but getting out of the six-foot hole is a lot tougher. Mitchell moves over to give me a hand, while keeping an eye on Randall.

"Don't even think about moving," he warns him.

Randall doesn't listen. He attempts to get up.

Mitchell grabs both of my hands and hoists me up. The second I'm out, Randall uses all his strength to lunge at me. We both fall back into the grave, the skull getting crushed under my back, causing jagged edges to dig into me in several places. Randall's knee is pressing against my neck, squeezing the air out of me. I dig my nails into his leg, but he doesn't let up at all.

"Get off of her now, or I'll shoot!" Mitchell yells, his gun trained on Randall.

With my hands on him, I can read his emotions. He wants to die. If he doesn't, his plan isn't fulfilled. I can't tell Mitchell that though because I can't breathe or speak.

Mitchell fires a warning shot, and Randall's body lowers closer to mine. I take the opportunity to ram my knee straight up into his groin. He groans but doesn't let go. This can only end in one way: with one of us dying.

CHAPTER TWENTY-FOUR

I know Mitchell doesn't want to shoot since Randall and I are a tangled mess of limbs and he could easily hit me. But if he doesn't, I'll die anyway. I try to meet his gaze around Randall's head. I need to do something to give him a better shot. I stop gripping Randall's leg and reach for a bone beside me. In one swift motion, I connect the bone with Randall's head.

He stumbles to the side, and Mitchell's gun fires. Randall's bloody body falls limp on top of me. "Get him off me," I say, my voice raspy.

Mitchell jumps down into the casket and pushes Randall off me. With the bullet wound in Randall's head, we don't need to check for signs of life. He's dead. "Are you okay?" Mitchell asks as I rub my throat.

I nod. "Chandler Evans," I manage to croak out.

Mitchell helps me up and lifts me out of the grave. Then he pulls himself out. I know he wants to make sure I'm all right, but we both know there isn't time. We search the headstones. Chandler Evans's grave is on a small raised area with more members of the Evans family. This time Mitchell drives the bucket loader, which I left running. He digs up the grave as I count the seconds ticking by. I can't sense if Pastor Evans is still alive or not.

When Mitchell hits the casket, he stops and jumps out of the machine. We dig out the edges and pull up the lid. Pastor Evans's eyes are closed. I press my hand to his neck. "There's a pulse, but it's weak."

Sirens sound, and lights illuminate the cemetery. Mitchell climbs out of the grave and motions to the officers and the paramedics.

"Pastor, can you hear me?" I say. "It's Piper Ashwell. The paramedics are here. We're going to get you out of here. Just hold on."

With oxygen filling his lungs again, he should be okay. If we'd taken any longer to find him...

Mitchell and I arrive at the hospital at 4:00 p.m. with a bouquet of flowers for Pastor Evans. Our entire day was busy with police reports and exhuming the bodies of the other victims from the cemetery. Losing six innocent people on one case is too much for me to grasp. I just keep trying to focus on the fact that we were able to save Pastor Evans. Not to mention Randall Williams will never take another life. He can't hurt anyone anymore.

Pastor Evans is sitting up in bed, looking better but still exhausted and pale. "Detectives," he says when he sees us. "I'm glad you're here."

I place the vase of flowers on the table beside his bed. "How are you feeling?"

DRASTIC CRIMES CALL FOR DRASTIC INSIGHTS

"Grateful, blessed, and heartbroken all at the same time." He takes a shaky breath and sighs. "I hired Randall. I was so set on trying to make everyone into a better person. I knew Randall had his faults. His last employer told me there was something off about him, but I was convinced I could show anyone the error of their ways."

He wanted more and more souls to save. It's not the traditional definition of gluttony, but that's how Randall saw it. He took some liberties with that one. But after being inside Randall's mind, I'm pretty sure he saw Pastor Evans as feasting on all his church members' souls. I shake the thought away, not wanting to channel Randall ever again.

"I'm sorry we weren't able to solve this case sooner. Your church lost a lot of good people."

"I've learned a valuable lesson in all of this. It is not up to me to judge my constituents. I can only show them the ways of the Lord and allow them to live their lives after that. Randall helped me see that."

I'm not sure how he's able to find good in all this death, but maybe that's what he needs to do to move on from it.

"Thank you both for saving me."

"We're just happy we were able to," I say. "Get some rest. You have a service to give in a few days."

He smiles and leans his head back on the pillow.

Mitchell and I turn to leave when Pastor Evans calls me back into the room.

"Ms. Ashwell, don't view your gift as anything but. We can't always see why we are meant to do something, but know it's part of a bigger plan. I don't know why God chose to save me and not the others, but I do know you were given this gift for a reason. Use it to the best of your ability. That's all anyone can ever ask of you."

"Thank you, Pastor." I swallow the lump in my throat that seems to come with every death I can't prevent.

Mitchell slings one arm over my shoulder, and for the first time, I don't shrug off the physical contact. "So, does this mean we have to start attending church on Sundays?"

"And risk you spontaneously combusting and burning down the entire place and everyone inside?" I shake my head. "I'm afraid it's just too risky."

"You're right." He opens the door to the hospital for me, and we step out into the snow showers. "I had another risky idea in mind."

"You're going to stop hitting on every pretty woman we come in contact with on these cases?" I scrunch up my face. "I don't know. That one might kill you, too. I'm just not sure you have it in you."

"I was actually thinking we go see a movie."

"A movie?" I stop walking and face him. "Is that a joke?"

He shoves his hands into his pockets. "No. I just thought neither of us gets out anymore. We're always busy with cases. And I'm pretty sure you've begrudgingly admitted I'm one of your friends. So, what the hell? Let's pretend to be normal people for one evening. We'll see a movie, pig out on popcorn and candy, and then I'll drop you off at home so you can call your dad and tell him how boring I am and how you can't see why any woman would ever date me."

"Hmm…I already know that last part, so what if we skip the movie and order in while watching TV on the couch with Jezebel?"

"You're going to read on commercial breaks, aren't you?" he asks.

DRASTIC CRIMES CALL FOR DRASTIC INSIGHTS

I smile. "Every single one. If I don't, you might try to engage me in conversation, and we certainly can't have that."

"No, we can't have that. People might start to think we were really friends and not just pretending to be."

"That would be awful," I say, looping my arm through his.

He looks down, and at first I think he's trying to make sure my right hand isn't in a position to read him.

"You're safe," I say, wiggling my gloved fingers and then putting my hand in my pocket.

"Somehow I doubt that. I'm pretty sure being friends with you is going to do me in."

"Eh, you're practically ancient anyway. The big three-oh and all that."

"I've had a good run."

"So, Chinese or pizza?" I ask as we walk back to his Explorer.

"We've barely eaten for the past week. I say let's order both."

"Keep talking like that, and we're going to get along just fine, Detective."

"Be honest. You keep me around for my amazing puns."

I let go of his arm and walk around to the passenger side of the Explorer. "If I'm being honest, one day I'm going to accidentally throw you in a ditch because of your puns. They need to go."

He opens the door. "Oh, come on. I have one for every case we work. I think that's pretty inventive of me. You know you're looking forward to the next one I come up with."

I get inside the car and close the door. "Start thinking

then, because we never have much time between cases, and I have a feeling our next one is just around the corner."

———

If you enjoyed the book, please consider leaving a review. And look for *Foresight Favors the Felon*, coming soon! You can stay up-to-date on all of Kelly Hashway's new releases by signing up for her newsletter: https://bit.ly/2ISdgCU

ALSO BY USA TODAY BESTSELLING AUTHOR KELLY HASHWAY

A Sight For Psychic Eyes (Piper Ashwell Psychic PI Prequel)

A Vision A Day Keeps the Killer Away (Piper Ashwell Psychic PI #1)

Read Between the Crimes (Piper Ashwell Psychic PI #2)

Manuscripts and Murder (Madison Kramer Mysteries #1)

Sequels and Serial Killers (Madison Kramer Mysteries #2)

Fiction and Felonies (Madison Kramer Mysteries #3)

The Day I Died

Unseen Evil

Evil Unleashed

Replica

Fading Into the Shadows

Into the Fire (Into the Fire #1)

Out of the Ashes (Into the Fire #2)

Up In Flames (Into the Fire #3)

Writing as USA Today Bestselling Author Ashelyn Drake

The Time for Us

Second Chance Summer

It Was Always You (Love Chronicles #1)

I Belong With You (Love Chronicles #2)

Since I Found You (Love Chronicles #3)

Reignited

After Loving You (New Adult romance)
Campus Crush (New Adult romance)
Falling For You (Free prequel to *Perfect For You*)
Perfect For You (Young Adult contemporary romance)
Our Little Secret (Young Adult contemporary romance)

ACKNOWLEDGMENTS

As always, thank you to my editor, Patricia Bradley. You always make my stories better with all your insights—no pun intended with this book. Big thanks to my family for allowing me to disappear in my office for hours on end to write every day. To Ali at Red Umbrella Graphic Designs, you always create the perfect covers for the series. Thank you for another gorgeous cover.

Thank you to my VIP reader group, Kelly's Cozy Corner, for sharing my work and being early readers. And thank you to everyone who picks up a copy of the book. I hope you enjoy Piper as much as I enjoy writing about her.

ABOUT THE AUTHOR

Kelly Hashway fully admits to being one of the most accident-prone people on the planet, but luckily she gets to write about female sleuths who are much more coordinated than she is. Maybe it was growing up watching *Murder She Wrote* that instilled a love of mystery, but she spends her days writing cozy mysteries. Kelly's also a sucker for first love, which is why she writes romance under the pen name Ashelyn Drake. When she's not writing, Kelly works as an editor and also as Mom, which she believes is a job title that deserves to be capitalized.

- facebook.com/KellyHashwayCozyMysteryAuthor
- twitter.com/kellyhashway
- instagram.com/khashway
- bookbub.com/authors/kelly-hashway